JUJU JUSTICE

JUJU JUSTICE

T.E. LANE

Published by IngramElliott, Inc.
www.ingramelliott.com
9815-J Sam Furr Road, Suite 271, Huntersville, NC 28078

Book design by Maureen Cutajar, gopublished.com
Cover design by Jeanine Henning, jeaninehenning.com

ISBN Paperback: 978-1-952961-36-6
ISBN E-Book: 978-1-952961-37-3
Library of Congress Control Number: 2025950348

Subjects: Fiction / Thrillers Suspense; Fiction / Visionary and Metaphysical; Fiction / General; Fiction / Family Drama; New Orleans; Voodoo; Magic

Published in the United States of America.
First Edition: 2026, First International Edition: 2026

For Ray and Pearl,
who never met a stranger and whose family
was their ultimate treasure.

*Only the whispers of the bayou that are
kindled with magic will wiggle their way free.*

PROLOGUE

The woodshed stands alone, but not forgotten. June Mae lies in her bed a half mile away and ponders a spell. This one is for, of course, love. What else is there? June wonders for a split second if she blew out the candles in the shed before she snuck home. A jolt of fear runs through her. She considers sneaking back out to double check, but it's too risky. Her mother, Alma, and sister, April, are both light sleepers. No, no. It's fine. She remembers blowing out the flames before returning home.

June flips the yellowed pages of her grandmother's old spell book. June knows the book is not for reading, though. She knows it was wrong to sneak into her mother's bedroom, lift the heavy quilt, quietly open the cedar chest lid, and rummage through old photos, the family Bible, and a coffee can of old jewelry, nothing worth much. Nothing worth anything. Except for her grandmother's old spell book.

Her mother, Alma, does not approve of the book, but she can't bring herself to burn the thing—although the old crones at the church believe she did so. June knows that Alma threw an old recipe book into the fire that day at the burning instead of the spell book. June wonders why her mother can't let go—Alma is certainly not a believer in what the book contains. Voodoo, hoodoo, juju—names for the unknown thread that runs through all of life. The electric thread that sparks love, hate, and all emotions in between.

The thread that can sew good, or, of course, knit evil. June sneaks another look at the love potion in the old book and makes a mental note to look for more black cohosh on her next scout into the woods. She must be careful, though, not to make the same mistake as before. The doll's-eyes she picked certainly looked the part. How was she to know it was toxic? Well, a little vomiting wasn't too harsh a price to pay to invite love into her life.

No, this time, she'd get it right, the love potion. And this time, it could bring her closer to the boy she likes. She closes the old book and stuffs it under her bed. It's time to sleep. And with love stories bouncing through the halls of her mind as she'll be bouncing through the halls of high school tomorrow, June falls fast asleep.

CHAPTER 1

It is a muggy day in the river bottoms of Louisiana. A crusty farmhouse sits on stilts—a relic that whispers of a lifestyle no longer relevant. The overgrown yard suggests a weary caretaker. Forsaken rosebushes litter a path to the river while lazy trees drip with Spanish moss. The ancestral low-country house is weathered with generations of history. Clearly, the structure is a testament to the craftsmen that labored its birth.

Inside the house, June Mae passes the old black-and-white photos tucked in a curio cabinet. As usual, she has a stirring in her soul. The yellowed images memorialize the lineage of a Creole family, churches, and landmarks.

She remembers gatherings in the woods, years ago, when she was guided by her father, Roy Mae, into the bayou. June remembers a bonfire flickering in the night, surrounded by a diverse circle of practitioners. Drums and rattles mix with voices chanting. Colorful storytellers share an intent to practice and preserve magic.

"June, we gotta go now." The loud voice of her sister, April, beckons her back to the present. "C'mon, we won't get a booth."

"I'm coming," June says, still lingering with the thoughts of the past. June has never been certain why all those evenings with her father and his unusual friendships set her on a path that would last a lifetime.

June checks her look in the hallway mirror. A skinny, dark-haired teen stares back at her. High cheekbones and dark eyes forecast a future exotic beauty. June sticks a lock of stringy hair behind her ear and bends down to adjust a clunky leg brace. The metal contraption holds a platform shoe in place on her right leg, which is a few inches shorter than the left.

From outside the open front door, April shouts, "June, get out here and help me and Mama."

June takes one last look at the photos of her ancestors. She reluctantly pulls herself away from the past, picks up a bag of tomatoes in the hallway, and rushes outside.

CHAPTER 2

The farmer's market is busy. Local farmers and artisans sell their wares to the community. June and April's booth is near the end of the market.

April huffs in annoyance. "I told you we should have gotten here earlier. We're at the end of the market, where nobody comes."

In the booth next door, a strange setup of exotic plants, tiny bottles, and straw dolls are helmed by a tall one-armed man known around town only as "Mister." His hair is a wild mess, and his brown skin glistens with sweat as he mulls over his potions and voodoo fixes.

"There's your friend," April scoffs and gestures to Mister's booth. "Most of the parish avoids the swamp witch."

"Yeah, until they need her," June replies and lifts a heavy basket of cucumbers onto their table. She follows April's gaze to Mister's booth. "And *he's* not my friend," she says. "He is the son of my friend."

Mama Moo, age unknown other than snow-white

dreadlocks, and her son, Mister, peddle potions, remedies, amulets, and curse-breaking spells up and down the Mississippi, under cover of darkness and in secret places. June wonders why Mama Moo sends Mister alone to the market every Sunday.

April raises her eyebrows and gives June a withering look.

"You look exactly like Mama!" June laughs.

April's fair skin reddens. She knows June is right—she is a younger version of their mother with curves to spare and freckled cheeks. June is the complete opposite in both appearance and nature. April finished high school two years ago and spends her days helping Mama in the garden and around the house.

The sisters get to work, setting out their mother's honey, jams, and vegetables. April is organized and fastidious about displays, while June absentmindedly lays out tomatoes. She fixates on one tomato and sets it on top of the cash box.

April fans away flies as a blond-haired, chubby teen boy stops at their booth. He unabashedly stares at April's bosom.

April reacts shyly. "Hi Billy."

Billy smiles and opens his mouth to speak, but Mister calls him. "Hey! Preacher boy . . . you better stay away from those Mae girls. One of 'em's a witch, and the other one's too old and way too much woman for you." Mister laughs loudly and lewdly grabs his own crotch with his one hand.

April is mortified. June shoots Mister a bird.

A passing group of teens join in the harassment. "Billy's got a girlfriend . . ."

Under the glare of the spotlight, Billy is compelled to act. He picks up two large, ripe tomatoes, one in each hand, and fondles them promiscuously while leering at April. The passing boys reward him with a hearty laugh.

April's cheeks grow red as she crosses her arms in an effort to hide her bosom. She turns her back and pretends to work.

The boy, known around the small town as "Bully Billy" due to his penchant for picking on weaker kids, laughs and heads for Mister's booth.

"Why did you let him get away with that?" June scolds her sister.

April ignores June's question. June follows Billy with her gaze and catches the eye of Mister. They exchange a menacing look.

An old woman passes by and pops Billy on the back of the head. "I'm gonna tell your father about this, young man."

Billy smiles insincerely. "Don't worry, Mrs. Johnson, I'll behave." The old lady gives Billy a stern look as she leaves.

Mister mutters, "Oh, you'll behave all right . . . right into her underpants."

June overhears this exchange and yells, "Mister, you better shut your mouth or I'm gonna tell Mama Moo that you are not selling her potions, that you're just goofing off with your friends!"

"Oh," a teenage girl passing by calls out. "These boys are gonna be in trouble with the swamp witch!"

Mister, suddenly venomous, yells back, "You stay away from my Mama!"

Billy becomes uncomfortable and walks away, back past the sisters' booth. April is bending over arranging jars. Billy looks over his shoulder, wiggles his tongue at Mister, and points to April's large rear end.

June has reached her limit. She reaches for the tomato on the cash box and throws it directly at Billy's face. It lands perfectly. His face is covered in red tomato meat.

April is appalled. Mister begins laughing uncontrollably. Billy's face reddens and he runs away.

CHAPTER 3

A silver sedan pulls into the circle driveway that graces the front of the Mae farmhouse. The only section of the overgrown yard that has the occupants' attention is the vegetable garden. Neat rows of plantings and tall tomato vines represent a main source of income for the family.

As Alma plops down on the tired porch swing, she inadvertently lets out a sigh of relief. Her bowed legs and sheer size make Alma appear older than her forty years. Alma wears a thin, tattered housedress.

The skinny preacher, Earl, and his son Billy exit the vehicle and walk up the porch steps. Earl sits across from Alma in a wicker chair that is often a roost for the chickens. He wipes off the chair next to him and pulls Billy down. Earl carries a black Bible under his arm and wipes sweat from his brow with a large handkerchief.

"Well now," Alma manages to belch out. "What brings you out this way, Earl?"

"Right, Alma, no small talk, I guess. Billy, here, has something to say to your girls." Earl gestures to his son, who is red-faced and mute.

April appears in the doorway carrying glasses of iced tea. As she passes out the much-appreciated refreshment, Earl nods and addresses Alma. "It seems you all haven't been around to church for a while, so first of all, how are you doing?"

"Oh, well, you know, Earl, things haven't been easy with Roy gone," Alma replies, taking a large swig of tea. "God rest his soul," she says. She dunks one finger in her tea and swirls the ice around. "What's the saying . . . if I had any luck at all, it'd be bad luck."

Earl thumps the Bible. "We all must put our faith somewhere, Alma. I put my faith in the good Lord."

Alma's eyes look toward heaven. Earl can't tell her intent. She nods politely but doesn't say a word.

Earl slaps Billy on the back and says, "According to Mrs. Johnson, Billy, here, owes April and June an apology for a little rough horseplay at the farmer's market yesterday."

A skunk runs out from under the porch and into the yard. "Pew-whee!" Alma shouts, waving a hand in front of her nose. Billy coughs and Earl covers his muzzle with the handkerchief.

April turns bright red and casts her eyes to the floor.

"April, where's your sister?" Alma says.

April shrugs.

Earl speaks softly, but with authority. "You know, Alma, there's rumors about your youngest spending time with that swamp witch. In fact, Mrs. Johnson thought she heard June spit a curse at Billy. If I recall correctly, your late husband also had a propensity for the river bottoms'—let's call a spade a spade—sinful indulgences."

Alma shoos away the flies that are trying to cling to parts of her sweaty body. She sees April retreat into the kitchen. "Come here, girl."

April reluctantly returns to the porch.

"Son, you got something to say," Alma says and nods toward Billy. "Say it. We'll pass it on to June."

Billy scratches his head and avoids April's gaze.

"Well, get on with it, boy," Earl spits at his son.

Billy never looks up but squeezes a faint "sorry" out of his lips.

Alma stands, dismissing Earl and his son. "Nice seeing you both, but me and April gotta get back to work."

Earl, taken aback, says, "I guess I'll be seeing you around."

As father and son depart, Billy sneaks a wink at April. She blushes.

Alma and April watch the preacher's car disappear. Under her breath, Alma mutters, "Sinful indulgences, my foot! Your father tithed every month. If the cards were treating him good, that church got a lot. He gave enough one time to paint the rectory."

At that moment, June emerges from the underbrush, singing an exotic chant. She carries a deerskin drum made by her father. June sees Alma and April standing on the porch. June can't shake the feeling that she just escaped trouble.

CHAPTER 4

The farmhouse is dark and heavy with too much furniture. The lights are off, and the kitchen table is lit by kerosene lamps. There's a banquet from the garden laid out for dinner.

Alma eyes June. "Preacher Earl and his boy came here this afternoon looking to apologize for something that happened at the farmer's market. Said old Mrs. Johnson heard you spittin' a fix on his boy, Billy. Is that true?"

June's eyes dart to her sister. April merely shrugs. Before June has a chance to answer, the wall phone rings.

April hops up and answers it. "Hello?"

"The stew is really good tonight, Mama," June says, blowing on a spoonful of vegetables.

In the background, April's only response to the caller is "uh-huh" and "okay." She hangs up and returns to the table, cheeks flushed.

Alma and June notice tears welling in April's eyes.

"Billy is really sick," April says. "That was Preacher Earl, and he said—"

Alma bangs the table with the butt of her dinner fork and shouts at June, "What'd you do to that boy, June Mae? You tell me now."

June swallows hard. Her eyes widen as her mother's gaze turns red hot. "I didn't do anything . . .you gotta believe me, Mama . . . I didn't do nothin'!"

"You did too!" April blurts. "You hit him upside the head with that tomato!"

June looks at her mother and shrinks.

"Preacher says everybody knows you're still visiting that old witch," April mutters.

"I've told you a hundred times not to mess with Mama Moo, June," Alma scolds. "She had your father under a bad spell too."

June is defiant. "You all might be satisfied with this boring life, but I'm not! I'm not gonna stop going. I'm good at this stuff, like Daddy was."

Alma slaps the spoon out of June's hands. "No dinner. Go to your room. I will deal with you later."

CHAPTER 5

It's late at night. Everyone sleeps except June, who wrestles with her thoughts. She remembers many nights with her father, laughing and spinning spells with Mama Moo. Those were some of the happiest memories of June's childhood.

June can't take it anymore. She nudges open her bedroom window and slips outside. She snakes her way down a familiar path to the riverbank. Through the underbrush, she sees a fire. She hopes Mister is not there. June doesn't know why he hates her so much, but it's always been that way. Regardless, she must see Mama Moo.

June, out of breath and frenetic, bolts into the crude campsite that she's visited so many times. Beyond the fire, a wooden river raft bobs in the current. The makeshift home sports sleeping pallets, food, and supplies.

Mama Moo, an ageless African-American woman with snow-white dreadlocks and piercing dark eyes, sits on a branch in a nearby tree. June spots Mister in the shadows. He skins an opossum. Blood, bones, and raw meat permeate the campsite's airspace.

"Preacher is blaming me for Billy being sick!" June cries, pulling her hair maniacally.

Mister laughs, but without mirth. Mama Moo jumps down from the tree, pulls out a brass bell, and rings it feverishly.

"I messed up real good this time, Mama Moo," June cries, ignoring the ringing.

Mister scoffs. "So, what's new, white pigeon?"

June wrings her hands. "I told them I didn't do anything, but I did!"

"What did you conjure?" Mama Moo asks, stopping the bell. She spits tobacco juice into the fire.

"I boiled a beehive in rabbit soup and injected a needleful into a tomato for prosperity. We need the money bad. Lights are off again," June whimpers.

Mister cracks a smile, but Mama Moo quiets him with a look.

"I set that tomato on the cash box to bring good luck. And that's the tomato I hit Billy with. He was bothering April. He's disgusting."

Mama Moo gives June a hard look. "Where did you get that idea for the tomato?"

"From you," June says. "You said the honey of a bee and the reproductive nature of a rabbit are certain to bring wealth."

Mama Moo considers this. "Were you sneaking around when I was talkin' to Jimmy Wilson?"

June's face reddens. She nods.

"You ornery girl!" Mama Moo chastises. "Tryin' to steal information that wasn't for you. This is what happens."

Mister moans in delight. "There she goes ... stealin' Mama's magic again. Only this time, it bit her back."

Mama Moo circles the fire and rings the bell like a serpent ready to strike. The energy settles.

Mama Moo shakes June. "Shame on you, girl. Stealin' magic that don't belong to you." She drags June to Mister's nearby skiff, bobbing in the water.

Mister trails them. "Where we goin', Mama?"

"You ain't goin' anywhere," Mama Moo replies. She jumps into the skiff and pulls June aboard. Mister fumes.

Mama Moo drives the skiff to the middle of the river and cuts the engine. She looks at June as they bob up and down. "You need to go home and sleep, girl. You did nothin' ... just because you have information, if you don't use it right, it doesn't do anything."

"But you told Jimmy—"

Mama grabs June's face. "Hear me good. Don't think you are more powerful than you are. If the information isn't yours to have, it can go sideways."

"What about Billy? Why is he so sick?" June pleads.

"That boy is sick because of what he does to himself," Mama Moo says. "Every time he crushes someone down, he's really steppin' on himself inside. Juju has its own form of justice."

Mama Moo pulls the cord on the motor. "You worry about yourself. I'm taking you home."

CHAPTER 6

Mister fishes on the bankside. He wipes his brow from the late-afternoon heat. In the distance he sees somebody coming, but he pays no attention. His eyes are fixed on the bobber floating on the water's surface. It starts to move. A nibble.

Mister jumps to his feet as the cane pole tugs at him. He struggles with his one arm as the fish pulls him toward the water. Suddenly, Billy appears at Mister's side. He grabs the pole and tries to land the fish, but it frees itself and escapes.

"Too big for that hook, Mister," Billy says.

Mister jerks the pole away from Billy. "Don't you ever grab at me again. You lost me that fish."

Billy takes a few steps back. "Okay man, relax. I was just tryin' to help."

Mister eyes the chubby teen up and down. He notices that Billy's skin is covered with red blotches. "You look like the one who needs help. What's wrong with your face? A spell, maybe?"

"Shut up. The school nurse says it isn't chicken pox. It's probably an allergy to something."

Mister grins. "Tomatoes, maybe?" He laughs maniacally and loads fishing gear into his boat.

Billy changes the subject. "I'm bored. What are you up to?"

"Thought I'd go explore down the river," Mister says and hops into his skiff.

As Billy turns to leave, Mister beckons him back. "C'mon. Let's go find a witch or two."

Billy looks dubious but hops in the boat.

CHAPTER 7

June tinkers in her conjuring shed. The dilapidated out-building is filled with jars of dried herbs, animal skeletons, and roots. June begins to blow out most of the candles that line the shelves. The sinking sun tells her it's time to go home.

Through the shed's small window, she is alarmed to see Mister's skiff rolling onto the bank. June freezes. She thinks about running, but it's too late.

Mister bangs the door loudly. "Come out, white pigeon."

Billy trots up from the skiff. He smiles uncomfortably as Mister points to the door. "Go on, Billy, kick it open."

Just then, the door opens. June is armed with a gardening hoe. "What do you boys want?"

"Just look at his face," Mister says and points to Billy's blotchy skin. "That's gonna leave pockmarks. Nobody's gonna want him. You owe him, witch," Mister snarls. "And we're here to collect."

Mister pulls a cigarette out of his pocket with his one arm and sticks it into his mouth. Once his hand is free, he lights it. The hot red tip of the cigarette burns brightly. The three look at each other, waiting for the next person to make a move.

Suddenly, Mister, with incredible strength, wrestles the hoe away from June and throws it yards away.

Billy freezes. June runs for the hoe. Mister sticks out a foot and catches June's short leg by the brace. She falls flat onto her face in the dirt. Mister looms over her. His cigarette dangles precariously from his mouth.

June flips onto her back and looks to Billy. "You gotta help me. He's the devil!"

Mister laughs and says, "Yeah, Billy, come and help her." The end of his cigarette snakes with hot ash. Mister flicks it at June's face. She dodges and the ashes land on the ribbon in her long braid, but she is unaware.

"She's all yours, Billy." Mister jogs to his boat. "I wouldn't touch that witch with a ten-foot pole." He jumps in his skiff and speeds away.

Billy looks at June. She is frozen with terror. He sees the ribbon in her hair begin to smoke. Without a word, he drops his pants and pees on her braid.

June is mortified. She sits up and screams. "What are you doing!"

Billy is speechless. He pulls up his pants and runs away.

June pulls her braid around and crinkles her nose at the smell. She runs to the river and dunks her entire head into the water.

CHAPTER 8

Alma pulls envelopes from her mailbox and stuffs all but one into her apron pocket, which she uses as a fan. She waddles back to the front porch as June emerges.

"All right, sleepyhead, 'bout time you got up," Alma says and plops into a rocker. "Don't suppose you're gonna tell me what happened last night? I heard you sneakin' in."

June shrugs and holds up a weathered wooden box.

"Where did you find that old thing?" Alma says, swatting away a fly.

June sits next to her mother. "In the bookcase in the hallway. It's filled with—"

"Yeah, I know, your father's postcards. His brother sent them from all over God's creation. He was a traveling salesman."

June flips through postcards in the box. Before she can ask anything more, April bops onto the porch in her Sunday best. She tosses a small white device into June's lap.

"You can have my MP3 player," April says. "I know yours is broken."

June looks up. "You broke it."

"No, I didn't," April says.

"Why are you giving June your player?" asks Alma.

"Devil's work," April replies. "Ms. Stillman says that secular music leads to sin."

June looks at Alma, who shakes her head. In the driveway, a minivan pulls up. Alma points to a basket of laundry that's neatly folded near the front door. "April, take Ms. Stillman's clean laundry as you go."

April picks up the basket and looks at her sister. "Ms. Stillman said to invite you to youth group because we're going roller skating. But I said you wouldn't want to go."

"Thanks for doing my thinkin' for me, April," June mutters.

April bounds down the front porch stairs and turns. "Ms. Stillman says if you keep foolin' around with voodoo, you're going straight to hell."

June's face burns in anger as April gets into the car.

June looks to her mother. "Not all voodoo is bad. I hate Ms. Stillman."

"Well, you can hate her all you want. Her laundry keeps the lights on."

June huffs and crosses her arms.

"Don't look at me that way," Alma says. "You bring most of this on yourself."

"Do you think I'm bad, Mama?"

"That mamaloi." Alma sighs and nods toward the riverbank. "I never understood what your daddy saw in all that. As if the gamblin' and drinkin' wasn't enough."

"But the magic . . . it calls to me, Mama," June says.

"That was your daddy's excuse, too." Alma rocks in silence.

"I think April's more interested in Billy than church," June says.

"April takes after my mama—a rule follower." Alma nods to the box in June's hands. "You, on the other hand, are more like your daddy. We wanted to go to all those places too. But I got pregnant with April. We had to move in with Mama and Daddy, and that kind of crushed your dad's dreams. He tried to be a farmer. But after my folks died, well, he just quit trying."

"Did you have dreams, Mama?" June asks.

"Yeah, when I was about your age, there was a hippie boy that worked at our farm for a summer. When he left, he gave me a book. It said there's a place beyond right-and-wrong thinking, where there's no fear, no judgment, where people are kind to each other. That was my dream. But I lost it."

CHAPTER 9

June bolts down the path to the river. A crow follows her overhead. She rounds the bend and sees the smoke from Mama Moo's campfire. As she tries to run to the fire, June falls to her knees and wails in distress. Her face is flushed. Her eyes roll up into her head so far that only the whites are showing. The nearby crow flies toward the fire and lands on Mama Moo's feet.

Mama Moo eyes the path as the squawking crow leads her along the riverbank to June. The teenager is barely breathing and has collapsed in the mud. Effortlessly, Mama Moo gathers June into her arms and, in the evening mist, seems to float back to the campsite.

Mama Moo places June so close to the fire that the girl begins to sweat profusely. June's eyes are wide open, but she is in a trance. June's eyes dart in all directions. Her arms and fingers twitch uncontrollably.

Mama Moo grabs her drum and begins to feverishly play and chant around the fire. She calls to her ancestors in an earnest prayer. "All my relatives, please find this child of spirit," Mama Moo wails to the sky. "And send her back to me."

The old woman feeds the flame with dry logs and stokes it until the fire dwarfs the entire camp. June begins to calm.

Mama Moo whispers, "Now that's good, child, all the elements of this earth are needed to lure you back to me." She anoints June's head with river water, throws dirt onto her feet, and fans her head with air.

After some time passes with Mama Moo's repeated feverish pleas, June slowly returns to herself. She becomes focused and gazes directly into Mama Moo's eyes.

Mama Moo whispers to June, "This was a voodoo attack. I don't know what kind of enemy you could have created to experience this, but may they be gone forever."

June is weak. "Tell me about the elements of the earth."

Mama Moo chuckles. "You just got back, my lovely little pigeon." Mama Moo mops June's brow with an old rag. "Time to learn later. Rest, child, rest."

From a high branch, the crow screeches loudly and flies to the north. A cacophony of harsh animal sounds captures Mama Moo's attention. Without warning, Mister trapezes down a nearby tree and hangs from his legs.

He holds a slimy snake in his teeth. With animal-like maneuvers, Mister spits the snake out, and the frightened creature slithers away. Mister removes a cigarette from his pocket and lights it with an impressive one-handed maneuver. He tosses the matchbook into the fire, which causes a firework effect, popping and spitting sparks into the air.

Mama Moo's bottom lip protrudes with a wad of chewing tobacco, which she spits into the flames.

Mister says, "Whoopee, white pigeon, still comin' after magic. I guess Billy didn't catch himself a witch after all."

June persists. "I don't care how much you try to fix me, I'm gonna keep coming until I learn all this stuff, Mister!"

Mama Moo looks suspiciously at Mister for a moment. A realization crosses her face, but she says nothing.

Mister jumps to his feet and stares at his mother. "I warned you about coddling this cripple with your secrets."

Mama jumps high in the air, seeming to pause in midair. June and Mister are mesmerized by her behavior. She slowly returns to the ground and sits by the fire. Instantly, the blaze is reduced to nothing but smoldering black ashes.

Mama Moo speaks in a strong voice. "I have my reservations about sharing anything with either of you."

Out of nowhere, she throws a heavy stick to each of them. "You will intuit a message in the ashes of the fire. You will thank the fire first and wait for spirits to answer. Pick a spot and write out the message in the ashes."

Mister puts out his cigarette and takes a seat next to the fire. Each word is punctuated with disdain. "Thank. You. Fire."

A dark shadow leaps from the ashes and forces its way into Mister's body. Overtaken, Mister covers his stick with ash and begins to write in the dirt: *Shame on you.*

A moment later, the shadow exits his body and returns to the ashes. Mister awakens from his trance and sees the damning words. He tries to scratch it out, but nothing happens. The words remain.

June watches this with trepidation. The stick in her hand trembles. June only manages to touch the tip of the stick to the pile of ash. A spark ignites and a word appears spontaneously over the ashes, written in flame: *Run.*

June doesn't waste any time. She throws the stick away, adjusts her leg brace, and scurries through the underbrush without looking back.

Mama Moo laughs uproariously as she watches June flee. Mister tries to get to his feet, but can't move. It is as if he has invisible chains holding him down.

Mama's gaze follows June as she disappears into the night. She turns to Mister, who is still trying to get up. His one arm won't function—he can't seem to lift his own weight.

"What did you do to her?" Mama says.

Mister knows better than to remain silent. "Teaching her she doesn't belong with us."

Mama Moo looks at her son. "That's not up to you, boy. I choose who to share my magic with."

Mister and Mama Moo lock eyes. There is an unspoken battle being waged, but neither utters a word.

Eventually, Mister backs down and his eyes find the dirt. "She ain't comin' back. You'll see."

Mama Moo spits tobacco juice into the ashes. "She'll be back. And soon."

CHAPTER 10

Three Years Later

Chiggers! Chiggers everywhere! June Mae, get back here, you, and finish the dishes!" bellows Alma Mae. Frumpy and middle-aged, she stumbles down the rickety back porch in pursuit of her agile seventeen-year-old daughter. "Don't go down there with 'dat mamaloi!" Alma continues, furiously waving a fly swatter in the direction of her younger daughter. "That swamp witch gonna fix you, girl. Sure as the day is long."

Now forty-three years old, Alma stretches out her flabby arm to snatch June's ponytail, which causes them both to stumble down the steps of the farmhouse. Alma, who wears a tattered satin slip, is halted when it catches on a nail in the banister. Seizing the moment of distraction as Alma frees herself, June scurries away into the expansive yard. Playfully, she taunts her mother by taking refuge behind clothes drying on a line. June pauses momentarily to adjust her cumbersome leg brace.

Alma gasps for breath at the exercise. Red splotches dot her pale cheeks and neck as she struggles to breathe.

June shouts, "Don't fall, Mama!"

"Don't fall my foot," Alma booms. "I'm gonna blister that skinny backside. You jist' git' your ornery self back here and help your sister now!" Alma raises the metal fly swatter like a weapon. This perpetual battle between mother and daughter has worn Alma to threads, and the words *just like her father* float through Alma's tired mind.

June, on the other hand, quickly recovers and seizes the opportunity to head toward the river. June knows the door to the birdcage is ajar only for a short time. In her efforts to escape, June pauses a second to look back, making certain her mother is okay. "Please don't fall, Mama," she mutters to herself. June runs in her awkward, uneven way toward the riverbank and out of sight.

Surrendering to exhaustion, Alma makes her way back up the porch steps. She shoos away a chicken and plops down into a wicker chair in defeat. The evening sun, also exhausted, lazily sinks below the horizon. "Show me a prettier place," she mutters, fanning herself with the fly swatter.

Alma surveys the family cemetery on the property. It appears less shabby in the dying light of the setting sun. Alma knows the cause of her wayward girl—her no-good father and all his wanderlust. June Mae is just like him—never satisfied at home and always on the lookout for the next entertainment. If Roy Mae wasn't in a gambling hall or a bar, he could be found in jail sobering up. Alma can almost make out his headstone from this distance. He's settled nicely into the family cemetery next to her kin. Now she knows exactly where he's at and where he'll stay.

"I managed to keep this place up the best I could, Mama and Daddy," Alma whispers toward her family buried in the cemetery. Refocusing on the absence of June, sadness trickles back into Alma's dreamless heart. She talks to her missing daughter. "You're just like that father of yours, June. No good can come from all this wanderlust."

The child in Alma pauses to reflect that perhaps she chose the wrong life. Lately, Alma's been belching up a weird sort of grief. The nature of this regret belongs to a person much older than herself. Alma shakes the feeling off. *Well, I've got to get up and do something.* As usual, she surveys the property with good intentions but does nothing.

"Chiggers everywhere," Alma repeats to herself. Alma sets down the fly swatter and grabs her weathered Bible. She opens it to a worn, bookmarked page. High above the house, a hawk watches with anticipation.

Through the kitchen window, Alma's oldest girl, April, watches this episode with disinterest and dries a plate. It's the same dance between Alma and her sister, June, day after day. The threadbare lace curtains play with the breeze as April's gaze follows her mother's labored breathing in the chair. April's mind wanders as she surrenders to her dish duties. Her only vision is of her boyfriend, Billy. The movie-date last weekend was one of their best.

From the porch, Alma catches April's blank stare and is immediately saddened. Her daughter is much too serious for a young woman, she thinks. Alma often ponders how the two sisters could be so different. She wonders—not for the first time—if she should have raised them better. *After all, they were both raised by me.*

April positions her curvy body nearer to the window in view of Alma. Her straight-backed posture flaunts an unearned sense of self-righteousness without one word of discourse. The curtains play with the spirited breeze as April reviews her mother with detachment. Her unwavering gaze toward the river catches Alma's attention.

Performing for the sake of April, who diligently continues her chores, Alma hurls the fly swatter toward the river and murmurs, "God has both blessed and cursed our life."

April rolls her eyes at this performance—she's seen it all before. In the end, June always wins.

Alma has survived her own wilted dreams, but warriors on for her children. She closes her eyes and whispers to no one, "Peace passes all understanding."

The clanging dishes bring Alma back to meet April's reproachful gaze. "Why do you let June run off all the time?" She holds up a dripping cup. "You leave me with all the work."

"Holy cow, don't talk to me like that, April. I mean it. I'll tie a knot in yer tail as sure as I'm sittin' here. I've managed to keep a roof over your head for all these years . . . the least you can do is chip in."

There's a moment of silence as April debates her next move. She folds. "Mama, I'm gonna make myself a pimiento cheese sandwich. Do you want one?"

"We just had dinner," Alma replies.

"Do you want one, Mama? I'm going to have one."

"Make me one, too, then. I've earned it," says Alma.

Alma reaches for an antique radio, which is already on, and cranks up the volume of the jazz station. She closes her eyes and sways to the sound, lost in imagination and feeling, just for a moment.

"Oh no," says April. Without hesitation, Alma breaks the spell and, following her daughter's lead, switches the channel to gospel music.

CHAPTER 11

The broken-down woodshed stands precariously at the riverbank, slumping as if tired from holding up the weight of the kudzu vines that envelop it. The thing's feeble wooden bones could be knocked down by a strong wind. The shed's one small window, a rough, square opening without glass, glows eerily with the light of a candle.

Mister approaches the shed, hoping the girl is still there. It will be so much more satisfying if June Mae can see—with her own eyes—the destruction of her little world. He has no idea why his mama has tried to teach the girl anything. She's a dunce. And a cripple. Of course, he has no room to judge—seeing as he's a one-armed, tough-skinned river rat.

Mister mutters to himself, "They'll see, one day real soon. I'm saving all the money I make at the bait shop for a golden arm. Well, maybe not gold, but metal. *Definitely* indestructible. Mama's voodoo dolls, hex potions, and juju jewelry are small potatoes. Paying the bills, barely scraping by—no, it's not for me. I'm gettin' out of this dump.

Everyone who ever told me I was worthless will regret it. Starting with Mama."

Mister quietly approaches the old shed. His heart swells as he peeks inside, hoping to get a glimpse of June Mae, but the shed is empty. He scoffs as he surveys the shed's contents—jars filled with herbs, bottles of liquids and animal bones, dried plants hanging from the ceiling. The girl is so stupid she'll probably poison herself one of these days. *Good riddance.*

Mister scours the ground for a stick and picks it up. He holds the stick up to the lit candle in the window and considers whether to move forward or whether to withdraw. After a few seconds, his choice is made. Mister pushes the stick forward and tips the candle over. Hot wax spills onto a pile of dried herbs, which instantly ignites. The flames don't take long. The fire consumes the shed in a matter of minutes.

Mister stands back and enjoys the fiery ball of destruction he has created. How he wishes the stupid girl were here to see it burn. This will teach her—and Mama too. He is the only true heir to the secrets of the powerful juju. The knowledge that his mama, known to all in the parish as the swamp witch, Mama Moo, should have saved for him and him alone. His birthright.

The shed burns brightly and, having easily consumed its fuel, smolders into a black pile of charcoal. Mister stomps out a few patches of grass that threaten to catch fire. He inspects his triumph and sighs in relief before heading back to the river raft.

So long, June Mae.

CHAPTER 12

June runs down the familiar river path. The rough under-brush pricks her skin but June never slows her commitment to freedom. She lifts her face to the sky and allows the sun and wind to caress her face. She dreams of traveling down the mighty Mississippi River to adventures unknown. Relishing the escape from her mother and sister, June immediately feels relief from the claustrophobic culture of the river bottoms—stagnated dreams, cruel gossip, and never-ending judgment. June suspects she'll miss things when she leaves home, but at the moment she can't imagine what.

June stops a moment to adjust her blasted leg brace and raised shoe. The thing was forever irritating, even with the elastic knee socks Alma had ordered for her from a catalogue. Satisfied, June stops a moment to take in the view. An African-American church congregation files into the water anticipating the cleansing ritual of baptism. Behind them, the sinking sun paints a final picture for the day in pinks, reds, and oranges.

Snatching juicy blackberries from a nearby bush, June watches the opposite riverbank as the faithful move slowly through the shallow water. Over the years, June has witnessed many baptisms, including her own, and never tires of the primal instinct to surrender to something greater. June squints her eyes nearly shut so that the murky water appears to consume the faces of the congregation. Their white clothing dances in the waves, creating ghostly apparitions.

As the crickets begin to sing their evening song, June spies a battered boat speeding down the river. The old skiff looks familiar to June, but she can't place it—it's helmed by a shadow. The driver rudely speeds past the church and leaves a wake that disrupts the congregation.

June has a strange feeling, watching the congregation dodge the speeding boat. She takes a last look as the skiff speeds upriver and continues on her journey.

As June rounds the bend, she stops short in disbelief. The stunned girl strains through the darkness to see the patch of hallowed ground—*her ground*—the site of her beloved conjuring shed. But it's no more. In place of the rickety woodshed stands a pile of burning rubble. It still smokes, but the flames that consumed it have vanished. June runs to the burnt mess and wails in anger. Tears roll down her face and she begins to hyperventilate.

June draws several long breaths to try to calm herself. Her heart breaks thinking of all she's lost—jars of dried herbs so lovingly preserved; that cohosh, which was so hard to find; the tiny, brittle bird bones; and the scraps of fabric that Mama Moo gave her for voodoo dolls.

As June turns to leave the ruined shed, she spies something

in the grass about a yard away. A matchbox, burnt on one side and empty of matches, lies in her palm. She flips it over and reads the logo—*Ray's Bait and Bottle Shop*. The bolt of recognition comes swiftly. The skiff. June knows for sure who was at the helm now. *Mister*.

Anger burns in her chest and causes a hot flush to creep up her neck and into her face. June says out loud to no one, "If Mister thinks he can stop me from calling on the juju, from learning Mama Moo's magic, he's got another think comin."

June screams in pain for another long moment. Once it's completely out of her system, she draws herself up again and makes a decision.

CHAPTER 13

June sneaks through thick brush along the river's edge. She can smell the campfire and knows she's getting close to Mama Moo's campsite. June is halted by the sound of distant chanting. "*Bah day Bah day, oh man hah ee! Oh, Bah day, oh way, ho man hah ee!*"

In spite of her leg brace, June threads herself with agility along the well-worn path, even in the dark. Creeping forward around the bend, she sees a campfire casting eerie shadows in the darkness. June can just make out the shape of the wooden river raft that she's visited many times before.

Studying the art of the spirit world with Mama Moo has been the highlight of her young life. It's as if she's drawn to the flame of this knowledge that frightens most people. She understands, though, that magic is like electricity—there is no wrong or right, only usefulness and intent. Electricity can burn you up or light up your world.

Tied to a piling nearby is the weathered skiff that June saw earlier. She can now read the logo clearly—*Ray's Bait and*

Bottle Shop—where Mister works. June notices a can of gas in the stern of the boat near the motor.

In the dark, without warning, Mister trapezes down a nearby tree and hangs by his legs on a large branch. Face to face with her predator, June's heart nearly stops. Frozen by terror, she stares as Mister swings closer—nose to nose, inches from her face. Too stunned to scream, June watches Mister dismount the tree as if he were a tiger on a hunt.

Within seconds, he fiercely grabs June's ponytail with his teeth and drags her—now the prey—to the water's edge. The young woman's body shudders with fear, yet June remains stunned and silent.

June's frightened mind suddenly registers that they are not alone. Mama Moo sits atop the floating river raft that she calls home, twisted in a freakish yoga position. In the misty darkness, the old woman seems to float a few inches above the deck.

Mister tosses June aside and arrogantly lounges on the weedy riverbank. With his one arm, Mister removes a cigar from his soiled shirt pocket and places it between his lips. He pats the pocket of his work shirt—embroidered with his name above the *Ray's Bait and Bottle Shop* logo. Finding the pocket empty, he sucks on the cigar, unlit.

"Told you I smelled somethin' comin'," Mister says to his mother.

Mama Moo sneers at them both and unwinds from her yoga pose. A frog croaks nearby. The old woman snatches the creature from the deck of the raft in a flash. It wriggles in her hands a moment before she drops it into a mason jar and screws the lid on tightly. "When you invade my space, uninvited, be ready for the consequences."

Mister laughs and stretches a toe toward the campfire. His toes are like fingers. He pulls a small twig from the fire and lights his cigar. Mister's eyes bulge in the firelight.

Mama Moo turns her attention to June, who lies at the edge of the river, near the raft. The stricken girl struggles to recover her wits. June feels the familiar pull to the old woman and has great respect for this root doctor. She recalls, as a young girl, her father telling stories of Mama Moo's knowledge with the herbs and healing.

June remembers visiting Mama Moo's camp for the very first time. She was only a small child, and her father carried June on his shoulders. June's mother, Alma, gave both of them a dressing down when they got back home. From then on, June visited the swamp witch in secret.

"You again?" Mama Moo finally says to June, dark eyes flickering in the firelight. The old woman offers the usual verbal abuse to her young protégé, whose passion for knowledge, so far, has superseded June's need for hospitality.

June sits up and turns to Mister, unable to hold back any longer. "I know it was you who burnt my conjuring shed. You think that's gonna stop me from comin'?"

"You ain't nothin' to me," Mister spits at June. "I don't know nothin' about no fire." Mister smiles, but remains a little uneasy.

June straightens her shoulders. "You work at Ray's, don't 'cha?"

Mister shrugs. "So what? A lot of people work at that old dump. What you sniffin' around here for?"

June gathers her courage and directs her answer to Mama Moo. "I'm gonna keep comin' until you teach me everything you know."

"The white pigeon comin' after Mama Moo's magic always! Why don't you give up?" taunts Mister.

Suddenly, Mama Moo spits tobacco juice in a huge arc that hits June's face hard, like a rock. This disgusting act causes June to lose her composure, and she wipes the brown juice from her face as her eyes water. This gesture gives Mister renewed courage.

June wipes away tears and says to Mama Moo, "If I'm not to know, then why do you whisper in my ear at night?"

Taking a long drag from his cigar, Mister casually asks, "Mama, what's the cripple babblin' about?"

Mama Moo smiles in amusement, but the smile never reaches her eyes.

June glares at Mister. "You ain't the only one she talks to, Mister. And you ain't gonna stop me by burnin' down my shed." June brushes the riverbed off her clothes in defiance. "Mama Moo tells me to collect graveyard dust, mix John the Conqueror root, and teaches me to uncross tricks."

Mister snaps his gaze to Mama Moo. "Mama, you told me I was the special one. That I was to be the next root doctor."

Slowly and deliberately, Mama Moo's eyes travel from Mister to June, assessing them both with discernment. Neither target moves under the spell of her powerful gaze.

"Mama?" questions Mister.

In an instant, Mama Moo leaps from the raft into the brown muck. She violently wrestles June into the shallow water. June writhes in pain and terror as Mama Moo shoves June's head under water and holds it tight.

The old woman's entire body weight leans on June's lungs, forcing out the last remaining particles of oxygen. Mama

Moo delivers a screechy, demonic laugh to the heavens. A moment later, Mister's baritone howl calls to the full moon, neither one heeding June's flailing limbs.

June's eyes bulge under the water as the darkness closes in. She feels her life force begin to leave her body. June's last fleeting thought is . . . *why?*

June's lifeless form lies drenched on the sandy riverbank. Mama Moo smiles down at the girl's limp body. Mister runs to Mama, then runs into the woods, and then back again. All the while, his arm wipes sweat from his forehead. He is in continuous motion and on the verge of panic. "You killed her!"

Mama Moo shoots Mister a warning look. "Don't you dare look so cockeyed when it was you who gave the verdict!"

"I didn't mean to—no, not this time," he says. He crumples to the ground in fear. "It's your fault!"

Mama Moo moves to Mister's side and gently strokes his hair as if he were a baby, cradling him in her arms. "Shh, now. Such robust words possess unlimited power, my son. Shh. Hush now. Just because you have acquired some knowledge doesn't mean you have wisdom," she soothes.

Suddenly, Mama Moo slaps Mister hard across the face. Mister's face reddens.

He slaps his mother's hand away. "I hate you, Mama."

Turning away in shame, Mister misses the slow smile that creeps onto his mother's face as she pulls a deerskin pouch from her pocket. Silently, she pulls a pinch of iridescent white dust from the bag and throws it at Mister's feet.

For a second, Mister is confused. He reaches down to touch the sparkling white dust on his legs, but before he can brush it off, a swarm of fire ants materializes on Mister's feet and legs. They bite his legs mercilessly. Squealing in pain, Mister bolts into the river and tries to slap the ants away.

Ignoring her son's curses, Mama Moo retrieves another pinch of the white dust from the bag and sprinkles it under June's nose. "*La Lumiere defait l'obsurite.*" She repeats the mantra in English, "The light defeats the darkness," chants Mama Moo with intensity.

Instantly, June bolts upright, gasping for air. She stares in horror at the face of Mama Moo. Mama Moo leans in very closely and whispers into her ear. "When you want hoodoo as much as you wanted that air, come back to see me, child," Mama Moo says with an eerie cackle.

June has had enough. Without thinking, June breathlessly swings her fist at the old swamp witch, but misses. Rage replaces fear. In one swift motion, June shoves Mama Moo to the ground, adjusts her leg brace, and moves quickly toward Mister's battered boat, bobbing in the current.

Before anyone can react, June pulls out the recovered matchbook from her pocket, lights the entire thing on fire with one of the remaining matches, and throws the ball of flame onto the skiff. Perfectly aimed, it hits the can of gasoline that June had spied earlier. The boat burns in a spectacular fireball.

The fire illuminates June's escape into the shadows.

CHAPTER 14

Fifteen Years Later

As she does every morning, June takes a moment, stops, and smiles at the sign hanging over the door of her eclectic French Quarter shop, *Miss June's Bizarre Bazaar*. June's happiness can be attributed to a feeling of belonging—and having a place where she can finally be herself.

Locals who know her place understand that, while the storefront facing the busy street offers tourist-friendly exotic items like animal bones, cloth voodoo dolls, candles, and jars of herbs, the *real* magic exists behind a hidden door disguised as a bookshelf. Through word of mouth, June has built up a successful practice, offering guidance, potions, curse relief, and other white magic services in her secret temple room.

In the distance, a boat horn from the river blasts its arrival into the port. June is startled by the familiar sound—it reminds her of home. The buzz of the French Quarter, as it always does, fills her with the joy of fully being alive. She takes a moment to reflect on the passion for her business, her escape from the river bottoms, and the peace that comes from knowing she's right where she's supposed to be. She muses on a thought: there's a genuine reason people call their life a journey. It's a passage, she thinks, from one place to another, yes. But it's also facing parts of yourself that you didn't know existed or that you didn't want to acknowledge.

Immediately, fumbling through a vintage forties handbag for the shop keys, June's thoughts leap unbidden back to the riverbank, to the smell of a campfire, to her head under water, to Mister's cruel sneer.

That night was a blessing and a curse. A curse because she nearly died. A blessing because it was the catalyst for change. The day after her high school graduation, June packed a suitcase and began her own journey. Taking odd jobs along the way, June spent a year backpacking in Europe. A months-long stint in Rome (with more than one passionate affair to remember) and a dangerous season in Morocco all helped June hone the knowledge of spiritual practices around the globe. Practices she's become quite an expert at and rituals that help weave together the meaning in her life.

Ultimately, though, it was a sweltering summer in Chile that got June thinking about home. Checking in, as she did from time to time, with April, June learned that Alma was ill, and April was married and pregnant. Due to a flooded airport, June didn't make it home in time for her mother's funeral. When she finally returned home, it only took a few days of April's anger to remind June why she'd left in the first place.

June had a feeling when she landed in New Orleans on her way back out of Louisiana that she needed to stay. She loved the ironclad streets filled with artists and vendors and tourists from all around the world. She loved it all, but mostly the feeling she got when walking the streets. They were never devoid of people and never silent of music. The whole atmosphere was mystical, and within a few days, she knew she would become part of the mystique. Her layover lasted another day, and another month, and another decade.

June pushes away the thoughts of the past and turns the key to the present. She'd let go of all of it when she turned thirty-two earlier in the summer. She enters the shop as the little bell fitted to the top of the glass storefront door jingles delightfully. June enters and breathes in the multi-layered spicy and floral scent of the shop that bring her back to her sense of optimism. This is her oasis, her salvation. She flips the sign on the front door to *Open* and smiles at the day.

CHAPTER 15

June checks her look in one of the shop's many wall mirrors. She wears a polka-dotted dress and tall beehive wig, a testament to her love of old movie fashion. For a split second today, though, she feels unnerved again because she sees Alma's reflection in the mirror. She recalls an old photo in which her mother was as young and beautiful as any Hollywood starlet wearing a similar outfit. June had been amazed. When she'd asked Alma about it, June saw a shadow creep behind her mother's eyes, and Alma had dismissed her with a command to finish her chores. June never asked about the photo again.

The front bell jingles and snaps June back to the present. She exits the bathroom wearing a smile. She sees an odd couple browsing a shelf full of small animal skulls. They are both dressed head-to-toe in New Orleans tourist gear—purple T-shirts sporting a Mardis Gras harlequin and loads of plastic beads—even though the celebrated event concluded months before.

"Greetings and salutations, dear friends," June says.

The wife smiles warmly at June. "Hello, Miss June. I've heard so much about you!"

June begins to respond but is cut off by a cough from the petite woman's husband—a robust man wearing a flat-billed cap sporting the city's professional football team.

The wife shushes him with a gentle touch to his big, hairy arm. "High Priestess, I've heard great things about you from the concierge at our hotel. He said you might be able to help us."

"I don't like this place," the husband whispers to his wife, gesturing to June. "Look how she's dressed."

Taken aback at the irony considering the man's own outfit, June wobbles slightly on a pair of thick platform shoes. Only she knows one of them has a hidden raised heel, helping to camouflage her shorter leg. Most of the time, June manages to ignore her "limb length discrepancy," as the doctors called it. Everyone else just called it a clubfoot.

Inwardly, June recoils at the memory of being taunted about her awkwardness by the children at school. Those memories never failed to surface when she stumbled or fell, even after all these years. Although her mother had spent every dime she could scrape together for June's surgery as a child, the deformity relapsed somewhat in later years. She could have another surgery now, but the fear of more pain keeps that decision on hold. It's easier for June to manage with lifts and special shoes.

Suddenly, the wife removes the husband's stiff, brand-new hat. "As you can see, my husband needs your help." She points to his shiny bald head.

June nods respectfully. "Of course."

Embarrassed, the man rubs his head self-consciously, replaces his hat, and wanders into a corner of the shop displaying ornate, carved wooden knives.

June smiles at the woman and holds up an index finger to indicate "just a minute." June deftly navigates the narrow aisles of merchandise, passes the display of voodoo dolls, and steps carefully on a short step stool. She grabs a white labeled bottle from the top shelf of a cabinet attached to the wall.

June hands the glass bottle to the wife. "I think you'll be pleased with this purchase." The wife motions for her husband to join, which he does. June continues, "This formula was given to me by a Native American shaman. I studied with him for a year. He was eighty-eight years old and still had a head full of long, luscious black hair."

Skeptically, the husband's eyebrows lift. The wife beams.

June concludes, "I believe you will be quite satisfied with the results. Instructions are on the label."

The wife smiles broadly and nods to her husband. He pulls out his wallet and the trio heads to the register.

Just then, a lovely young woman enters from the back of the store and waves to June. She approaches the register. "I'll finish 'dis for you, Miss June." Violletta speaks with a Haitian Creole accent and sometimes mixes English with her native language.

"Thanks, Violletta." June returns to the shelving unit and adjusts the remaining bottles and jars.

As the couple exits the shop, the wife turns and waves. "Thank you, Miss June!" She jabs the husband in the ribs. He raises his hand goodbye with a scowl on his face.

June approaches Violletta who stuffs the transaction receipt into a drawer. "So . . . I decided on a dress!"

June picks up a feather duster from behind the counter and commences dusting jars of herbs. "You picked the spicy one, didn't you?"

"Yeah, the short, beaded one is amazing." Violletta pulls up a picture on her phone.

June smiles widely at Violletta. "Trent will love it."

June reaches into a basket of sweetgrass near the front window. She ties the long strand into a bulky knot and hands it to Violletta. "Hang this over your wedding bed. Guarantees a fruitful union."

Violletta smiles shyly. Her caramel skin blushes a little. The front doorbell jingles.

A booming, beautiful voice carries through the shop. "Let's get through the wedding before we worry 'bout the honeymoon, eh?"

June and Violletta look up to see Pearl, Violletta's aunt and a woman with a mighty presence. She hands a covered basket to Violletta.

"Thanks, Aunt Pearl," Violletta says, sniffing the basket. "Warm cornbread. Oh no—you take this cornbread, Miss June, or I won't fit into this dress!"

June accepts the basket with glee.

"There's plenty in there for the both of you to get you through the workday. I brought your favorite, the cornbread, but there's some fried green tomatoes in there too. They're especially for you, Miss June."

"Pearl, are you trying to fatten me up?" June says, pulling out a corner of hot yellow cornbread and swallowing a chunk. She moans in delight.

"Absolutely," Pearl says, heading for the door. "A man'd

have to shake the sheets real hard to find either of you girls in bed."

And with that, Pearl smiles at the ladies and departs. June and Violletta eagerly dive into the basket of goodies.

CHAPTER 16

A former commercial chicken coop emerges from the underbrush. It's a large, long building with a variety of cars parked near two double doors. Unadvertised and known to the local clientele as The Coop, the establishment has seen better days. However, its current patrons are only interested in what goes on inside.

Surprisingly, the dull building outside is transformed into a lively den of iniquity inside. At one end, dog and cockfights entertain groups of gnarly guests. At the other end, a brothel invites the varied patrons to partake in both drugs and sex. Across the entire front wall, a long, elegant wooden bar sports towers of top-shelf liquor in front of a lighted mirrored wall.

Overseeing all the action, Mister emerges from his back office. Now in his late thirties, his teenage wildness and animal-like demeanor have disappeared and have been replaced by the complete opposite. He is now a polished businessman, well-groomed and wearing an expensive suit. Mister also sports an intimidating metal prosthetic arm. Mister oversees his empire with the pride of a conquering industrialist.

An alluring green-eyed young woman hangs on his arm. The woman strokes his chest. "I'm so proud of you, M. Who'd have thought when I first met you at that dive bar, you'd end up owning such a classy place?"

Mister smiles in remembrance and looks down at the woman. "Lucky Lucy's Bar was the only place that'd let this ole' swamp rat in back then." He snorts with a mix of sadness and pride. "But I showed them. They should all see me now."

Lucy looks around the building. It's a weekday afternoon and not packed like the weekend nights, their busiest times. Even so, there are a few dozen patrons at the poker and craps tables in the center of the expansive space. Velvet curtains line the walls of the industrial-sized building and the space has been transformed into a plush environment to accommodate gambling, boxing, dancing, and lounging sections.

Mister looks at Lucy. "Bringing you with me was the best decision I ever made." Mister kisses her. "And who'd have thought when you served me a drink at that dive bar, you'd turn out to be my right hand, girl." He holds up his flashy metallic prosthetic and chuckles at his own weak joke.

Lucy laughs a bit too hard but halts as the front entrance, a set of tall double doors, swings open and allows the afternoon sun to flood the dark interior of The Coop. A towering, silver-haired man with dark, olive skin enters the building, trailed by two burly bodyguards, one with an eyepatch and the other with spiky bleach-blond hair. The silver-haired man carries the aura of power with his walk as well as in his elegant appearance.

Lucy quickly scuttles away toward the back office, the beads on her short cocktail dress swishing. "I'll be in the back finishing the liquor order."

Mister turns to the new arrival and removes a Cuban cigar from his pocket and inspects it carefully. "You did good with this batch, Judge. Your old cronies in Cuba are still paying off, I see." Mister runs the cigar under his nose, inhaling deeply. "We've already sold out of the boxes you delivered from Cuba last week," Mister says.

"I told you I'm a good business partner, didn't I?" Judge Armand Royale boasts and pats Mister on the back.

"I wasn't expectin' you until tonight," Mister says. "We have somethin' special lined up for our favorite, most honorable judge." Mister gestures to a set of female twins dressed identically in shiny silver minidresses. The ladies bend over a mirrored table and snort two lines of cocaine.

"Looks great . . . but I'll need a raincheck," Judge Royale says, shaking his head. The judge leans closer to Mister and whispers, "Pearl's got pictures of you and me doin' business. That son-of-a-bitch PI followed me here last week." The judge sighs heavily. "You need to *fix* this before we're front-page news."

Mister shakes his head. "I don't need to put a voodoo fix on that PI. My boys will simply encourage him to leave the county." He hands the unlit cigar to Judge Royale, who lights it. "But I do need more cemetery dust, pronto."

The judge takes a deep drag. "Pearl's got a restraining order. You know that Haitian bitch. Until the divorce is final, she's got me locked out. Cemetery is off limits to me, but I decided to put your kid Abraham on it."

Mister's eyes flash with anger. "What are you sayin'?"

"I'm saying that Abraham owes me money too. I called in a favor from your boy to settle his debt. He's like a cat; he can get in and out real quick without anybody noticing. He'll bring us more cemetery dust and we're back in business. *¿Tú entiendes?*"

Mister flexes his metal prosthetic fingers menacingly. He pinches the judge's red-hot cigar cherry between two metal fingers and snuffs it out. "You got some big balls, Judge. That Jamaican belongs to me. He doesn't piss 'less I say so."

The judge looks at his wilted cigar and breathes deeply, puffing out his chest like a gorilla in attack mode. Anger rises silently between the two men as they face off, eye-to-eye. A few surrounding patrons stop what they're doing to watch.

Mister is aware of the attention. Suddenly, he laughs loudly. In an instant, Mister retreats back to the role of gracious host and nudges the judge in the ribs playfully, but a little too hard.

Judge Royale is not amused. "*Pequeña perra,*" he mutters under his breath.

"That boy's gambling debt to me needs to be settled before Abraham goes gettin' on any other pony," Mister says with a forced smile.

"Let's not forget who keeps your ass out of jail," the judge replies venomously.

Mister fumes for a moment but does not react. He is well aware they are being watched. He removes an envelope from his pocket and slyly hands it to the judge, who peeks inside to see a thick wad of hundred-dollar bills.

"Your cut from last week's sales," Mister whispers. "Includes cigars, dust, and protection."

"Good boy," the judge says with a condescending pat on Mister's shoulder.

Mister's smile instantly fades. He forcibly removes the judge's hand from his shoulder and runs a metal finger down the judge's cheek. An angry red line appears on the judge's face.

The judge's bodyguards flank the men and wait for a signal. For an instant, all the action in The Coop ceases. All eyes are on Mister and Judge Royale. Hostile energy seems to create its own atmosphere around the two men.

Finally, a little fear creeps into the judge's eyes. The older man cracks a smile. Mister softens. The action in The Coop resumes. The pissing match is over . . . for the moment.

CHAPTER 17

June wipes the counter in her dark voodoo shop. She approaches the front door to lock it up for the evening. On her way, she adjusts a display of Miss June's Bizarre Bazaar magnets and smiles at the thought that these trinkets—a small skull, a tiny voodoo doll, and a white prayer bow all stamped with the store's logo—adorn refrigerators around the country, maybe even the world.

As she turns the lock, she is startled by a Jamaican woman wearing a bloodstained chef's apron stamped with the logo for Pearl's Kitchen. Behind the distressed woman lurks a young man dressed in hipster clothes. He resembles the woman.

June opens the door and beckons them inside. "Hi Maxine . . . Abraham?" June says with hesitance.

Maxine wrings her hands. "Miss June, I'm sorry to catch you at closing time."

June nods, concerned.

Maxine continues. "My boy and I need some help."

Abraham stares at the shop floor, not meeting June's eyes. Although dressed in trendy jeans and a jacket, his demeanor is that of a child in trouble.

Maxine pinches him with attitude. "Where's your manners?"

Abraham reluctantly looks in June's direction and nods hello. June smiles warmly at the young man.

"God sure has a way of showing you the truth through your children," Maxine says with a sigh.

June leads Maxine and Abraham to a bookshelf at the back of the store. June pulls a book down like a lever and a hidden door is revealed. The trio enters a small temple room.

The room is decorated with altars and religious icons. It is lit by candles, and each corner of the room holds an offering, such as money, bones, and amulets. On the walls are written the names of voodoo gods: DIEUDOONEZ, SINDIORDOCORE, and ELA SOBO. Sets of strange eyes are painted on the ceiling to ward off evil. Unlike the lighthearted atmosphere of the shop, this room exudes a powerful energy.

June ties a ceremonial handkerchief around her head and sits on a cushion in front of a nearby altar. She invites Maxine and Abraham to join her.

"Lucifer himself got a hold of my boy," Maxine professes.

Abraham scoffs. "Mama . . . you know I don't believe in this shit." He turns to June and quickly adds, "No offense, Miss June."

Maxine slaps the back of Abraham's head and pretends to spit over her shoulder. "Show some respect, boy."

June puts a finger up to quiet them. She breathes heavily to center herself. "Abraham, you have linked yourself to the dark side of things. I know the unsavory one you serve. Very risky pleasures."

June jumps up, grabs a nearby jar of cornmeal, and draws a circle around the three seats before sitting back down. "When dealing with Mister, I am gonna need some help from the ancestors and the unnamed ones."

June places her hand on Abraham's head and effortlessly dispels a Haitian Creole blessing. "*Kite m 'limen lanp ou a, di zetwal yo. Li pral retire fènwa a alantou kè ou.*" June lifts her arms to the heavens and repeats the blessing in English. "Let me light your lamp, say the stars. It will remove the darkness around your heart."

Abraham looks at his mother, longing for this to stop. "Mister tried to use this hoodoo on me, too, Mama. If you're payin' for this, pay this lady for some good luck instead. Then them cards would be sweet on me and I'd be free of this mess."

Maxine pinches his arm hard. Abraham squeals and yanks his arm back. "You see what's happenin' here, Miss June? All he can think about is the gambling."

June nods in silence. Abraham jumps up from his seat to leave. Maxine pulls her son back to the cushion on the floor.

"Not only that," Maxine continues. "Last night, this boy showed up at home covered in mud and scratches. Says the judge has him doing a nasty job, but won't say what."

Abraham squirms uncomfortably. "Mama, hush. I can't have Mister knowing what I'm doing for the judge. They are in a pissing match."

Quickly, June grabs a twig lying near her seat, snaps it in half, and sticks it under Abraham's nose. He is immediately sedated by the aroma and sits slumped in a daze.

"Maxine," June whispers, "you must trap a squirrel that lives near The Coop. Understand?"

Maxine nods in agreement.

June continues, "Remove the squirrel's brains and heart. Make a milk and garlic stew. You should both be facing east. You eat the heart, while Abraham consumes the brains."

June reaches for a wooden box on the altar. She removes a small packet of translucent white powder and hands it to Maxine. "Add this to the stew. After eating it, Abraham will puke his guts out. But he will also be puking out the desire for gambling. Or, you will puke it out for him. It's up to the spirits."

Maxine's eyes widen but she pockets the cemetery dust with a nod.

"After you are done, bury the killing knife with a give-back," June continues. "Take locks of Abraham's hair and place them with the knife at the foot of the tree where you found the chosen squirrel. Understand, every second is of in-finite value, for his life is being lost, minute by minute."

Maxine looks worried. As Abraham stirs back to con-sciousness, his mother drags her son to his feet. "That devil, Mister, is sucking my boy down the drain."

"I agree. Probably best to exit through the back alleyway," June says. "Eyes are always watching."

Abraham staggers toward the door in confusion. June waves smelling salts under his nose and he perks up.

June says, "Don't worry, Abraham, the effect will wear off in a half hour."

"I'm not afraid of that one-armed thug," Abraham slurs. "Or that old Cuban judge."

"With a mother like Mama Moo, you best be very afraid of Mister," June warns. "And Judge Royale has connections in high places around this town. You should steer clear of both of them."

Maxine pulls on Abraham's sleeve. "You need to shut your mouth, son."

June responds, "The only courage that matters is the one-moment-to-the-next kind." Still holding the wooden box, June opens it and grabs a pinch of the cemetery dust between her fingers. She paints a cross on Abraham's and Maxine's foreheads. "May the light be with us all."

Maxine offers June a bundle of money. June pushes it back into Maxine's hands. "Reward comes when we don't have to watch life from the shadows. Now, go. Hug the darkness through the back exit and down the alley. No one must know you've been here."

CHAPTER 18

It's a bright new day. April Mae steps awkwardly from a cab, straightens her posture despite her weight, and dusts herself into a proper attitude. She wears a modest, loose-fitting housedress. April looks at the shop and the sign reading *Miss June's Bizarre Bazaar.*

April examines a postcard from her purse and says to the cabbie, "This can't possibly be correct."

From inside the grimy yellow cab, the driver says, "In thirty years, I've never got an address wrong. It's the best juju shop in the Quarter. That'll be thirty-eight-fifty."

"My bags?" April asks, annoyed. The cabbie huffs and exits the car. Straining in the heat, the cabbie unloads April's five large suitcases and mops his brow with a sleeve.

April wipes a stream of sweat from her forehead and fishes for exact change, in bills and coins.

Annoyed, the cabbie shoves the change into his sagging pockets. "*Salope de touriste bon marché,*" he mutters in Creole. Then shouts out the window in English as he speeds off, "Rent a truck next time, lady!"

Drenched with nervous perspiration, April kisses her gold cross necklace and clutches her purse close to her chest. Turning toward the strange shop, it takes April three trips in and out to retrieve her bags from the sidewalk.

Once inside for good, April spots an unusually short but muscular man leaning against the glass counter. He wears a paint-splattered tank top and reeks of too much cologne and testosterone.

April fights a wave of dizziness as he lights a cigar. She hacks loudly.

The shop's pretty Haitian cashier, Violletta, approaches from the back storeroom. She plucks the lit cigar from Jay's fingers and throws it out the front door. "No smokin' in the shop, Jay. You know that."

"Hey! That was a Cuban," Jay wails. "You owe me, girl." Jay shrugs and moves toward the register.

"Excuse me, I'm looking for Miss June Mae," April says to Violletta.

The cashier sticks out a hand. "I'm Violletta, I work with Miss June. What time is your reading?"

"June Mae is my sister," April croaks. She is overcome with heat and swoons with dizziness. She dabs her forehead with a handkerchief retrieved from her sleeve.

Jay watches with detachment. Sensing Violletta is distracted, he pops open the cash register and pockets a twenty-dollar bill.

Violletta reaches over the counter and slaps his hand. "Jay, put it back or I'm gonna tell June."

April staggers. Violletta steadies her as Jay pockets the twenty.

Jay comes out from behind the counter. "Lady, are you okay?"

April is white. Within seconds, she crashes to the ground, taking a crowded display of shop wares with her.

CHAPTER 19

Jay's tiny efficiency apartment sits above Miss June's Bizarre Bazaar. Its light source comes from twin balconies—one in the front overlooking a busy tourist street and one in the back, with a private courtyard view.

April slowly regains consciousness. She is sprawled across Jay's bed. Cracking open her eyes, April sees her own reflection in the mirrored ceiling. She is spread-eagle and naked except for her matronly white bra and panties.

April screams. A shirtless Jay nearly spills a piping cup of black coffee.

Mortified, April scrambles to cover up with a blanket.

"Cajun throwdowns can be a bitch, huh sweetheart?" Jay laughs and carries the coffee to April.

April sits straight up and presses her legs tightly together as she surveys her surroundings. She pulls the covers up to her chin as she notices erotic paintings littered everywhere around the apartment. On the bedside table, she notices a set of barbells. She grabs a small one and hides it behind her back.

"You were out cold, sweetheart," Jay continues. "Head hurt? I mighta' banged you around a little gettin' you up the stairs." As he grabs a box of pastries from the counter, Jay whispers in French Creole, "*Les accidents arrivent, hein, grosse salope?*"

April is clueless to his meaning: *Accidents happen, huh, fat bitch?*

He pushes Creole coffee and beignets toward a groggy April. "Air's broke. It's a real stinkhole in here."

April shrugs off the refreshments while cocooning herself in the quilt. "Where am I?"

"Above the voodoo shop," Jay answers. "Is Junebug really your sister? Cause there's no resemblance." Under his breath, he mutters, "*Je veux dire aucun, génisse (I mean none, heifer).*"

Aggressively, Jay shoves the powdered sugar delights so close to April's face that it leaves white powder on her nostrils. As he goes to wipe it away, she screams hysterically.

"Hey lady!" Jay yells. "Shut up! Shit, I was only wiping your nose, *trust me.*" He shoves the beignets again. "Café Orlean's finest. A friendly chick scores 'em for me. I just thought your blood sugar might be low 'cause you fainted. I think you might like 'em. C'mon, sweetheart, try one!"

Exasperated, April asks, "Who are you?"

Through the open window, several alley cats screech loudly. April overreacts and grabs Jay, then recoils.

Jay laughs. "Take it easy. It's only cats." He yells out the open French doors, "Shut up, freaks!" He grabs a dirty sock from a pile on the floor and wipes his forehead. "It's freakin' hot in here. What the fuck? If you can't take the heat, stay out of the Big Easy, right sweetheart?"

April faints. Jay shakes her hard, but she's out cold again.

"Hey lady! Wake up! Don't do this!" Jay nervously babbles in his native French Creole again, "*Réveillez-vous! Ne fais pas ça!*" Jay tries to pry her eyelids open. April doesn't budge. Jay slaps her too hard.

April does not respond.

"Wake up! C'mon, lady! I didn't do anything!" Jay tries to shake April awake. He gives up and pours himself a whiskey.

CHAPTER 20

eturning home from work dressed in a fifties hoop skirt and blonde wig, an exhausted June clunkily climbs the stairs to her third-floor flat. As she's climbing up, Jay bounds down from his second-floor efficiency, and pretzels June around his waist. June is at least a foot taller than he is. "Take me on up to my place," she whispers.

As Jay easily carries June up the stairs, the chemistry between them is apparent. "I'll take you up to the penthouse, alright," Jay says.

June crinkles her nose. "You stink."

"Yeah, the air's broke," Jay says, hiking June farther up his body.

"You said you'd look at it today."

"Too busy, baby. Didn't have a minute," Jay replies. As they reach the second-floor landing, Jay says, "Baby, you gotta' swear you'll never get fat. Swear it, Junebug. Swear!" He playfully twirls her around to the point of nausea.

June yells, "Stop! Stop it! Jay! Please!" Jay sets her down.

She adjusts her leg brace. "And stop calling me that. I hate that nickname."

Through the open door to Jay's apartment, April bolts up, instantly awake. She sees Jay molesting June's breasts in the hallway. June playfully pushes Jay away.

"Leave. Her. Alone!" April booms. Her voice echoes like a shot through the narrow hallway, completely stunning June.

June stares at her sister. It takes her a moment to process what she sees. April is wrapped in a blanket from Jay's bed. This simply does not compute.

June shakes her head in disbelief. "April?"

"It's okay," Jay interjects. "I was babysitting your sister all day. She fainted in your shop, but she's fine. I didn't do nothing."

June looks from Jay to April, stunned into silence.

CHAPTER 21

June's top-floor flat is a moody mix of the ancient and modern—Southern gothic meets monastery. The Zen-like vibe of the simple furnishings and peaceful décor is marred by only one eyesore—a tasteless, ornate, claw-foot bathtub perched like a throne in the middle of the living room. June's twin balconies—one in front overlooking the street and one in back overlooking a central courtyard—mirror Jay's apartment below.

April soaks in a bubble bath, eyes closed. Her pale shoulders are the only body part that isn't covered by the soapy water.

A jittery June flits around the apartment, manufacturing unnecessary tasks, like straightening mindfulness and crystal healing books on a shelf.

"You're makin' me nervous," April says, opening her eyes and mopping her brow with a washcloth. "Stop scratchin' around the room like Mama's skanky cat on that rusty old tin roof."

"Sorry about the heat, air broke yesterday." June stops fidgeting and looks out the back balcony doors to the midnight sky. "Do you recall how miserable our ole' clammy room was back in the river bottoms, and how we'd sneak down to the river to go skinny dipping to cool off?"

"Well, let's just say I remember sweltering, but I never went skinny dippin', I assure you," April says, correcting her little sister.

"Uh huh," June smirks. "Are you sure?" She grabs a folding fan and steps out onto the balcony. The courtyard appears magical in the moonlight, like a set from a Tennessee Williams play.

June breathes in the night air and stretches her shoulders, trying to relax.

"Must you leave the doors open?" April calls out. "Someone will see me."

"No one can see anything. We're on the third floor," June says and shakes her head. "Just look at that moon . . . the stars . . ."

April huffs and eyes June through the open doors. "Really? Must you?"

June rolls her eyes.

"Shut the door. Right this minute!" April barks.

"Relax, April," June mutters. "I just need to cool off a minute."

From the courtyard below, Jay's shrill voice wobbles through the thick night air. It's clear from his slurred speech he's had a drink or three. "Junebug! Get your fine ass down here now!" Jay yells. "*Je vais te faire du bien* . . . I'll make you feel good, baby."

June grins down at Jay. She wishes for a moment alone.

Somewhere out of sight, a chorus of alley cats screech in awful harmony and glass shatters in the back alley.

"Shut the hell up, you stinkin' strays or I'm gonna bust your heads open!" Jay bellows into the night.

"June! Please shut the door!" April squeals from inside. She tries to cover herself with a frothy layer of bubbles. "That ridiculous buffoon actually saw me in my underwear! He *undressed* me. Did he tell you, Junebug? The audacity of it all. It's too much to bear."

June offers no response from the balcony. She continues to admire the inky night sky.

"Well?" April implores. "Just what do you intend to do about my violation?"

After a continued moment of silence, April mutters, "Well, nothin' I suppose. I can see you're gonna take his side."

Outside, the heat rises in June's face, matching the sweltering temperature. She takes a deep breath and attempts to control her temper. She almost chuckles at the absurd notion that—after all this time, after all she's accomplished, after breaking away from her past in the river bottoms—her sister can still piss her off.

"April, that's real ugly talk," June says, sticking her head into the apartment. "And please don't call me Junebug. You know I've hated that name ever since Daddy took it up."

Stunned, April responds, "Me? You're chastising me? Unbelievable. You never did take my side in anything. *Ever.*"

June opens her mouth, ready for a fight—a familiar old feeling that she's happy to revisit. Before she can, however, a loud knock startles both women. June steps into the living room and heads toward the front door.

April squirms with anxiety at her nakedness in the tub. She reaches for the towel on the bed, but it's too far away. "Don't open the door! It's that jackass!"

June throws her sister a judgmental look, but not a towel.

In the hallway, the shop's cashier, Violletta, hands June a fatigued backpack. "You left this downstairs," she says. "Also, Maxine's here. Says it's urgent."

June looks toward April, who has shrunk down into the tub. Only April's eyes are visible above the bubbles, like an alligator trolling the bankside for prey.

"I'll be down in a minute," June tells Violletta with a flip of the head toward April in the tub. Violletta nods in understanding and retreats back downstairs.

April emerges from the water and wipes soap from her eyes. June tosses the weathered military-style bag on the bed, and a huge wad of cash spills out. April's eyes widen at the sight of the money until a shadow passes through her peripheral vision. April splashes water on her face.

April's gaze follows the shadow, which looks vaguely like a smoky version of a man wearing a fedora. Before her eyes can focus, the shadow disappears out the French doors.

Oblivious to this incident, June stuffs the cash back into the bag and tosses it in the apartment's large walk-in closet.

A teapot whistles from the kitchen. Steam hisses into the atmosphere.

"You okay?" June asks April, making her way toward the angry pot.

"Yeah," April responds. "Just thought I saw—"

"A ghost?" June interjects. She pulls teacups from a cabinet.

"A shadow," April replies.

"People say the spirit of Tennessee Williams hangs around from time to time. This used to be one of his houses."

"Rubbish," April says. But her face reflects an uncertainty that amuses June.

June hands April a cup of tea. April declines with a gesture but June presses the cup into her sister's soapy hands, now pruned from soaking too long.

"You're gonna want that," June says. "It's got a little extra somethin' on board to calm the spooks."

Behind June, April sees the shadow pass again, but June doesn't. April sniffs the tea.

"I'll be right back." June heads toward the front door. In a mirror near the entryway, June spies April sip the tea and spit it out.

"Drink up," June says, grabbing the shop keys from a hook. "It costs a fortune, comes from China."

"China? Yuck!" April complains. But when she sees the smoky shadow cross her field of vision toward the balcony again, she gulps it down.

As June closes and locks the door behind her, she mumbles to herself, "Take it easy tonight, Tennessee."

CHAPTER 22

The shop is closed and lit only by streetlights outside, giving the interior an eerie glow. June meets Maxine near the shop's front door. Her face is tortured with tears.

Maxine wears a bloodstained apron stamped with the Pearl's Kitchen logo. She hands June a bloody package marked *Chicken Livers*. "From Miss Pearl."

"Thanks, Maxine," June says. "Are you okay?"

"It's Abraham," Maxine replies. "My baby got arrested last night for breakin' into Pearl's cemetery, for dust. I'm goin' to butcher those junkyard dogs."

"Mister and Judge Royale?" June says. "Did you feed Abraham the squirrel stew like we talked about?"

Maxine shakes her head, no. "There was no time. I'm afraid Abraham has kissed the devil. The demon dog, Mister, is making my son pay off his gambling debt with all kinds of shady deeds. And now that dirty judge has his hooks in, too, forcing Abraham to steal from Pearl," Maxine says. Maxine has a murderous demeanor.

"Do exactly as I say and stay far away from both men, do you understand?"

Maxine nods, her anger barely controlled.

"Get three white eggs from three very white chickens," June instructs. "Write Mister's name on one, Judge Royale's name on the second, and the district attorney's on the third. Break the eggs on the courthouse steps just before the hearing."

June retrieves a tuft of green leaves from a nearby display. She hands them to Maxine.

"Sage leaves?" Maxine asks.

June nods. "Write the names of all the apostles except Judas on the leaves. Put them in your shoe. Sit directly behind your son at the hearing."

"Which shoe?" Maxine asks.

"Left one, heart side." June removes a gold necklace from around her neck and hands it to Maxine. "For power and protection."

Maxine inspects the dainty gold cross engraved with June's initial, *J*. Maxine nods and clasps it around her own neck. "You gotta fix that Mister," she pleads. "He's robbin' mothers of their babies."

"Go home now, Maxine," June comforts. "Follow my instructions and have some faith."

CHAPTER 23

As June returns to her apartment, April snores, asleep in the tub. June tiptoes past her sister to the back balcony. Outside, in the surprisingly cool midnight air, June takes in the enchanting courtyard below. Jazz music from a nearby club softens her mood. She watches a random couple romantically kissing under a lamppost beyond the courtyard.

Jay exits the building, stark naked except for a beret. He carries an easel, sketch pad, and box of charcoal pencils. Jay spots June on the balcony above and opens his mouth to speak, but June shushes him with a finger. She motions toward her apartment.

Jay vexes their encounter with provocative and lewd gestures. Out of April's sight, June promotes the foreplay by seductively undressing for Jay's pleasure. The mood turns lusty.

Jay scribbles on a pad and shows it to June. *You + Me = Later.*

June throws him a kiss goodnight and goes back inside, feeling a little lighter.

June enters her large walk-in closet, which resembles the prop room for a theater group—wigs, costumes, and orthopedic shoes line the shelves above a floor safe. Jars of bones and rare herbs sit, labeled and orderly, high on shelves for safekeeping. She punches a security code into the safe and pulls the door open. A substantial amount of money can be seen. She deposits the cash from her backpack and locks it with a click.

As June exits the closet, she sees April floating face down in the tub. "Oh my God!"

June runs to her sister and turns her over, trying to pull her out. She screams and slaps April across the face. "April! April! April!"

Suddenly, without warning, April wakes and slaps June across the face. Both women look stunned. Without a word, June hands April a robe and helps her clamber out of the tub.

April ties the silky robe around her body. She caresses the fine material. "My, my," April swoons. "This robe makes me feel downright luxurious."

"Silk," June offers.

"Never had anything this nice in my whole life." April sighs.

"Keep it."

"Generous," April says, "but not exactly appropriate for a preacher's wife. You see, I'm not supposed to lust after expensive things, let alone have 'em."

"I'm certain the treasures received from years of simply serving are priceless," June says.

April doubles over with laughter. Her strange overreaction leaves June confused and nervous. Almost as suddenly, April flips from laughter to a dark sneer. She circles June like an animal.

"Bullshit! Bullshit!" April hisses. "That's *Grade A* bullshit! Your head's not working any better than mine. Do you actually believe half the crap that spills out of your mouth, *Priestess June*?" The sisters share a long, hateful stare.

"Let's get some air, April."

CHAPTER 24

The streets of New Orleans buzz with life as June maneuvers April through the crowd. Their mood is a bit lighter.

"This place makes me feel things," April says.

"Like what?"

"Downright alive," April says, taking in the colorful sights. "I can see why you love it here."

June nods hello to a group of singing tourists as they pass by, waving at the sisters.

"How long have you owned the shop?" April asks.

"Let's see," June recalls, "I created it, uh, right after I moved here. Over a decade or so, I guess."

"So, you *created* it?" April asks, raising her eyebrows. "My, you created it. Of course you did."

June rolls her eyes. "I didn't buy an existing business, is all I meant. That would've been easier. Give me a break, April."

"Well," April says, "you must know, Mama would crow to anyone—everyone—back home about her little June. How her youngest had traversed all four directions of the world and how her baby journeyed to New Orleans to open a souvenir shop for tourists. Wonder how she'd have felt about a tawdry voodoo shop?"

The two sisters pause their verbal combat for a moment to watch a silver street artist change poses.

"Well," June replies, "it's kind of a tourist shop, in a weird way. For Mama's sake, I might have shed a little different hue on things. It's not important. Mama's dead. And today, matter of fact, I sold my shop. I turn the keys over in a few days. We have a lot to celebrate."

"Are we celebrating Mama dying, selling a scary voodoo shop, or our blistering reunion?" April retorts.

June pulls out some cash and violently throws it into the street artist's tip container before facing April. "I don't remember sending you an invitation."

April's mouth is a hard line. "And did I need to send you an invitation to your own mother's funeral?"

June takes off, moving as quickly as her leg brace will allow. April huffs indignantly and labors to keep up pace amid the crowded street.

June steps off the busy sidewalk onto the patio at Pearl's Kitchen. The homestyle food restaurant, a renowned New Orleans staple, is bustling with activity. Late-night diners choose between inside and outside seating.

April arrives a moment later and plops into a patio chair. June is already seated on the patio. A few other patrons dine al fresco and enjoy the pleasant evening.

April pants. "Invariably runnin' off, leavin' me behind. Nothing ever changes."

Violletta appears at their table. She wears a serving apron and name tag. "How you feelin' after that knock on your head?" Violletta asks April with a sweet smile.

"A little crazy," April answers, confused by Violletta's presence as a server.

"Crazy is contagious in the Big Easy," Violletta continues. "Everyone's as mad as a hatter. Somethin' to drink?"

"Violletta works evenings for her Aunt Pearl," June says to April. She smiles at Violletta. "Cajun tea, thanks, and make it a double."

"Water, please," April says.

As Violletta heads to the kitchen, June crosses her arms in a defiant posture and glares at April.

"I can always tell when you're pissed, little sister," April says, not meeting June's eyes. "It's sincerely not nice to be so disagreeable after I've come so far for this reunion." April meets her sister's eyes. "No need to wrestle your noisy thoughts all alone. Why, it must be like hell living in that brain of yours. So, you sold your shop, huh?"

"Why are you here, April?"

"I just gotta know," April says, eyeing June with suspicion. "Are you really laying in that little thug's bed? He's even got mirrors on the ceiling! Be sure your sin will find you out."

"Unless you want to sleep on the street," June replies coolly, "I suggest you refrain from spittin' Bible verses my way."

Violletta drops off a basket of bread. June inhales the sweet scent of cornbread and biscuits, trying to calm herself.

"Alright," June declares, "let's do this. Why not? Jay's my friend and he takes care of me. We use my bed, the one you're gonna be sleeping in tonight. Why are you here?"

April throws up a hand to stop June from sharing more. "Don't disgust me. And why shouldn't I come to see my only sister?"

June replies with a little less edge. "I don't like the mirrors either. In my world, mirrors are used in conjuring."

Alarmed, April repeats, "Conjuring?"

"Don't worry, the mirrors in my apartment and shop are clean and shielded. Feel absolutely free to use any of them anytime. So, really, don't fret, Sister, you're safe from evil."

April slams her fist so hard on the table that she sends silverware flying. A few patrons stir uncomfortably. She shouts, "You condescending, self-righteous bitch. Just because I'm a preacher's wife with six kids from a poor parish doesn't mean that my head is completely up Jesus's ass." April pulls a twenty from her bag and shoves it across the table at June. "Now, young lady, you will coddle me with the same respect as you do your payin' customers."

June stares at the twenty-dollar bill. The moment is palpable. "First of all," June replies in a low, controlled volume, "you can't afford me. Secondly, I can't imagine you'd be interested in anything I have to say. I believe your exact words were *savage at heart*. At least that's what I remember from your last letter."

Interrupting the tense moment, Violletta delivers a new set of silverware and dresses the table with a tray full of food—collard greens, corn on the cob, pork chops, and fried green tomatoes. April's eyes widen at the spread. Her attitude softens. June notes her reaction.

"Thanks, Violletta," June says.

"We didn't even order," April observes. "I guess they know you pretty well, huh?"

Both ladies begin to eat like it is their last meal. April watches June stuff her face.

After a moment, June stops eating and takes a breath. "I am hungry. Pearl's cooking is as good as Mama's, huh?"

April smiles at her sister. "Maybe we do share some DNA after all." April sits back and polishes off a cornbread muffin. She wipes her hands clean on a cloth napkin. "So, why did you sell your shop . . . seriously? Seems like there's a boatload of money coming in."

June smiles. "Why, April Mae! You're a preacher's wife. I thought you weren't supposed to be motivated by money."

"Well," April shrugs, "here in the Big Easy, I'm a tourist. Don't you get to be someone else on vacation? You're always dressing like someone else."

June considers this for a moment. Finally, she raises her tea glass in a toast to her sister. "Here's to being someone else."

They clink glasses and enjoy the meal.

CHAPTER 25

Mister's gambling den—The Coop—is in full swing. Music, drugs, fights, and escorts litter the scene. Mister surveys his empire. Satisfied, he takes a break in his private office.

Mister mixes a cocktail at the wet bar. His office is a tasteless, overly decorated dark room with couches, a desk, a safe, and shelves of unspecified voodoo paraphernalia. On the walls hang a collection of African masks. In the corner, an altar has been set up with black candles, a skull, and various voodoo dolls.

Lucy lies on the couch. Her sparkly cocktail dress is soiled with vomit. A cold cloth rests on her forehead. "I'm sorry I ruined the new dress."

Mister shrugs. "I'll get you a new one. Drink this." He hands Lucy a glass of thick, green sludge. "I mixed it up for you special."

She sits up and sighs heavily, dubious about the concoction. With Mister's urging, she sips it gingerly. "Baby, the last one didn't work. I'm still having these stomach pains every day."

Mister downs his cocktail in one gulp. "Don't worry, *ma petite fleur*. I won't rest until I figure out who put this fix on you."

Lucy considers her reply. After a moment, she ventures forth. "Maybe I should go see Miss June again? She really helped me last time. It was before I met you."

Mister freezes. He turns and stares coldly at Lucy, martini glass in his metal hand.

Lucy realizes she's made a grave error and downs the entire potion.

Mister crushes the martini glass into smithereens before heading back to the action.

*   *   *

In the main room, Mister resumes his host duties. He smokes a cigar and motions for Clyde, a curly-haired young man sporting colorful tattoos, to join him.

"Go get the swamp witch," Mister says.

"Oh no, boss," Clyde replies with a shake of his head. "Remember what happened last time? Mama Moo's hoodoo is scary. Frank's tongue was never the same. He still talks with a lisp."

Mister doesn't say a word. He stares a hole through Clyde.

"On my way," Clyde says and exits through the double doors.

Mister spots Judge Royale sitting at the bar with his arms around a slender redhead in a silky red dress. As Mister heads toward the bar, the double doors slam open. Clyde is back—with Maxine in tow. She is red-eyed and angry as a snake. She jerks her arm away from Clyde's grip.

"This bitch was spittin' juju on your place, Mister," Clyde says.

Maxine recognizes Judge Royale and walks defiantly over to him. She stares into his eyes, then looks toward the floor and spits on his shoes. "May the power of the axe fall on your head."

"What the fuck!" Judge Royale lifts a hand, about to pay Maxine back for her trespass.

Mister intervenes. He steps between the two and stops the judge's hand two inches from Maxine's face. As he stares down the intruder, Mister notices the gold chain hanging from Maxine's neck, and rips it off. He snarls as he recognizes the gold cross embossed with the letter *J*.

"The white witch sent you?" Mister demands.

Maxine's eyes tell the truth, although she doesn't speak a word.

CHAPTER 26

June and April exit Pearl's Kitchen and step into the balmy night. June eyes her sister as they amble through the French Quarter. A light breeze caresses them, and soft notes of nearby music waft through the atmosphere.

"So, April," June says, "are you going to tell me the *real* reason you're here?"

April takes in the sights around her and replies without looking at June. "We haven't seen each other in years," she says. "I just thought we could spend some time together." The night buzzes with life and April soaks it all in.

June walks around a street musician. April stops to listen for a moment and throws a fiver into the woman's violin case.

"April, I'm just . . . well . . . it's a bad time for me. My back is against a crumblin' wall."

"Time is evaporating all right, and I'm . . . what I'm tryin' to say is . . . you're my only sister, June, and I do love you."

June looks at her sister, touched by the sentiment.

"Whatever you came here to find," June replies, "I'll help. You're not sick, are you?"

"Unlike these misfits you surround yourself with"—April gestures randomly to the city streets—"I don't require your help. I've simply come to—"

"How did you get so damn miserable?" June interrupts.

"I'm not miserable," April counters. "I'm just not as astonished by life as you've always been."

"Really, April. Why are you here?" June presses.

April stops walking and turns to her sister. "I brought you a gift."

CHAPTER 27

June wakes in the middle of the night and clutches her elbow. It throbs with icy hot pain. She creeps out of bed carefully, trying not to wake April, who snores loudly. As June reaches the front door, she doubles over and grabs her stomach. Still, she doesn't make a sound. In agony, June steps into the hallway and quietly closes the door behind her.

June moans in extreme discomfort. Barely making it into the temple room behind her shop, June grabs her knee and collapses to the floor. She feels a white-hot poker in her knee-cap. A few seconds later, her shoulder erupts with stabbing pain. June's entire body is tormented.

At the same moment, across town at The Coop, an inebriated Mister performs for a group of customers. Mister stabs a small cloth voodoo doll with pin after pin. The doll has so many tiny pins it looks like a porcupine rolled over it. The audience laughs with every stab, although unaware that the doll—with brown hair—has one leg shorter than the other. Mister twists a gold chain wrapped unceremoniously around the doll's neck.

In the temple room, June twists in agony and drops to the floor. June hugs her body and crawls toward her voodoo altar. Fumbling, she reaches for a cloth voodoo doll, one of many in a basket. Without hesitation, June fiercely rips off one of the doll's arms. She removes a silver stick pin from a jar, dips it into the wooden box that holds the translucent white cemetery dust, and stabs the one-armed doll in the head.

At The Coop, Mister's performance is interrupted as his head explodes in pain. For a moment he cannot move. The audience—a mix of drunk gamblers and escorts—laugh at what they perceive to be a joke. Mister clutches the voodoo doll and runs outside. His audience halts their laughing and return to their mischief.

Outside, breathing heavily with anguish, Mister pulls the pins from the doll and unwinds June's gold cross necklace. Acknowledgment crosses his face as he looks at the doll. It's clear that June's power now matches his own. Instantly sober, Mister throws the doll into the distant woods.

In the temple room, June rises from the floor. Her pain has lifted. She clutches the one-armed doll and removes the pin. She tosses the doll into a trash can. The battle has ended in a truce. *For now.*

CHAPTER 28

The next day, April and June walk in the late-afternoon sunshine with a mood much lighter than the day before. The sisters meander the exotic streets of the French Quarter.

"Somethin' about New Orleans makes me wanna' eat all the time. Look at those pralines," April says, peering at the candy displayed in a confectioner's shop.

"We'll buy you a box to take home," June says. "By the way, when are you—"

April interrupts. "I'm really hungry. You say Pearl's biscuits and gravy are the best in the Quarter?"

June nods. "Yep, she serves brunch all day long on Sundays. There's many a night I've enjoyed breakfast for dinner at Pearl's."

The sisters round the corner and pass the alley next to Pearl's Kitchen. Strangely, the entire staff is gathered outside. Suddenly, June notices sirens in the distance, growing louder. June is alarmed and scans the crowd for Pearl.

When she doesn't see her friend, June pushes through the kitchen staff, followed by April. The workers stand in a silent circle. June gasps when she sees what they are staring at. Maxine is dead, lying face up near the kitchen door in a pool of blood.

April gags as she notices Maxine's face covered in earthworms. The worms wriggle in and out of every orifice. June kneels by Maxine. April recoils and removes herself from the scene to a nearby bush, where she pukes.

June is horrified to see that Maxine's bloody right wrist is now a handless stump. A crimson-stained meat cleaver lies next to her body. June inspects Maxine's neck to find that the gold cross necklace June had given her is missing.

June looks oddly at Maxine's severed arm, then realizes Maxine's hand is missing. It is nowhere to be found.

Pearl approaches from the kitchen with an egg and exchanges a knowing look with June. Pearl gives the egg to June, who places it carefully in Maxine's remaining left hand.

At the bushes, April wipes her mouth, recovering. She rejoins June and points to the egg in Maxine's hand. "What is that for?"

"It's a juju practice," June says. "If an egg is placed in a victim's hand, the perpetrator will be found quickly."

April swoons. "I gotta sit down." She wobbles to a nearby bench.

"I've never seen anything like this before," Pearl whispers to June. "With . . . the worms?"

June nods. "This is voodoo revenge. A few days ago, I was helping Maxine protect her son, Abraham, from dark forces. Mister must have found out and didn't like it. I think the missing hand is a message for me."

"What do you mean a message for you?"

"I made a mistake by underestimating Maxine's pain and fear," June says. "I suspect she confronted Mister."

Pearl wrings her hands, clearly upset.

At the curb, the police arrive and begin to secure the crime scene. Pearl sends her staff back inside and whispers to June. "I'm worried about Abraham. Maxine told me he was in jail. My ex-husband, the judge, and Mister are like Siamese twins—they're in bed together in more ways than one. They'll be worried that Abraham will spill his guts about all the dirty deeds they got him doing."

June nods. "One thing's for sure. Abraham's in trouble too."

Pearl heads to the street and meets the officers. June looks through the mounting crowd of law enforcement and finds April, nauseous, still sitting on the bench.

June grabs her sister by the arm. "April, let's go home."

April doesn't resist.

CHAPTER 29

Mister sits alone at the altar in his office at The Coop. A ceremonial black robe billows around his shoulders, and an African mask sits upon his head, donning the painted face of a demon. Over the flame of a burning candle, Mister holds a vial containing black liquid. His metal prosthetic hand feels no pain. With his free hand, he adds a pinch of white translucent dust to the liquid. The black liquid glows dark purple for a moment, then turns clear.

"*Détruis mon ennemi,*" Mister whispers. "Destroy my enemy." Removing the now-clear and cursed vial from the flame, he screws the cap closed and nestles the potion in a wooden box of Cuban cigars.

Moments later, in the main room of The Coop, Mister hands the box of cigars to Clyde. "This goes to the judge. He's waiting outside."

Clyde nods and exits through the double doors. In the parking lot, he delivers the tainted cigars to Judge Royale, who rides in the back seat, window down. The judge nods to his bodyguards in the front seat and they speed away.

CHAPTER 30

Leaving the chaos in the streets behind, June and April drag themselves up the stairs to the apartment. June stops short. "Go on up to the apartment," she tells April. "I want to make sure the shop is locked."

"You can't leave me here alone!" April squeals. "Not after all that mess today!"

"Don't be ridiculous," June says. "I'll be right back."

Before April can argue, June is gone.

Inside the darkened shop, everything appears to be in order. June yanks on the front door, making sure it's locked. She breathes a sigh of relief, which is short-lived. From upstairs, she hears April scream. June bolts toward her sister up the stairs, knocking over several merchandise displays with her urgent exit.

On the third-floor landing, she finds April collapsed in front of her apartment door. Jay, also having heard the scream, arrives at the same time. They both stare silently at June's apartment door. Above the threshold, nailed to the wall, is Maxine's bloody, severed hand.

Jay labors over an unconscious April. As he struggles to lift dead weight, Jay mutters, "*Vaca gorda*. I'm gonna drop the heifer." Carelessly, Jay knocks April around as he struggles to wiggle himself and April through June's apartment door. His rough treatment begins to wake April from her fainting spell.

June steps toward them. "Be careful; let me help."

"Back off, you're gonna make me drop her." Jay throws April onto the bed like a heavy sack of rocks. He wipes his brow. "How many times can this fat ass faint? Jesus, I've already worked out today."

June shoves Jay out the front door and into the hallway. "Go home."

In the hallway, Jay gags upon passing the bloody hand, still nailed above the door. "This is some heavy shit," he mutters. "Jesus, Joseph, and Mary!" Jay disappears down the hallway back to his second-floor apartment.

June runs back into the apartment, grabs a towel, and carefully removes Maxine's bloody hand. Before she can reach the freezer, the shadow of a man crosses the ceiling and disappears into the corner. June shakes the towel-wrapped severed hand at the spirit. "If you're hanging around, I could use some help here."

April stirs back to life on the bed. "Okay," she says groggily. "I'll help."

June shakes her head and plops, exhausted, down beside her sister. "I'm not talkin' to you, April. Go back to sleep."

CHAPTER 31

Judge Royale and his two bodyguards sit in the judge's black SUV in the parking lot of the county jail. The spiky-haired blond bodyguard sits in the driver's seat, idling the engine.

From the backseat, the judge hands a cigar box to the bodyguard who sits shotgun. The man inspects the box with the eye not covered by a black patch.

"Deliver this to Tony in the kitchen," the judge orders. "He knows what to do. Make it quick."

The man nods in obedience and exits the car.

CHAPTER 32

The next morning at Pearl's Kitchen, April and June scarf down an enormous breakfast. April wears an outfit that she's been repeating since she arrived—a loose-fitting, modest housedress. Her appearance is drab compared to June, who wears a retro-sixties minidress and headwrap.

"Please tell me you're not playing with the devil," April asks her sister. She pushes around scrambled eggs with a fork.

"Old-fashioned thinkin', April," June answers, then sips her Cajun coffee. "Magic, hoodoo, juju—whatever you want to call it—is a tradition as old as creation."

A young waiter refills their coffee cups. He wears ear, nose, and lip rings. The women are startled when he speaks. "Voodoo has a dark angel and a light one," he pronounces. "It deserves respect, same as any other spiritual tradition."

Both April and June look at the man. They are stunned by his interjection.

In response to their chastising glances, the man's cheeks grow red. "Or at least, that's what my old auntie tells me," he concludes with a grin.

The two women quietly sip on their coffees for a moment. The waiter disappears.

June lowers her voice. "Guess we always were a bit loud, huh?"

April chuckles. "Well you were."

"Yeah, anyway. As I was saying, voodoo is nothin' more than a way to cope with the spooks that show up in all our lives, right, April?"

April considers this but doesn't relent. "Spooks, maybe, but I deal with them another way. There's nothin' in the King James Bible that requires body parts and animal organs for salvation."

"But there is sacrifice," argues June. "What about Abraham and Isaac?"

"Yes, true, there is animal sacrifice," April hems. "But as for humans, well, the angel of God stopped Abraham."

"From sacrificing his *son*," June retorts. "That was God's original request, in case you forgot."

April, now cornered, huffs loudly. "June Mae, I'm talkin' about the blessed bloody hand on your front door! What the hell is goin' on?"

At April's escalating tone, restaurant patrons eye the pair suspiciously.

"Keep it down, April," June scolds. "Maxine's been a client for ten years. Her son is mixed up with depraved people. They were sending him a message, that's all. No devils, no demons."

"But it's with voodoo? Or whatever you call it?" April asks.

"No," June responds, "just human evil. Watch the news if you don't believe me."

April rolls her eyes and finishes her cup of coffee.

June continues, "Look, no tradition is so black and white as to be all evil. Maxine couldn't watch Abraham suffer, so she turned to a spiritual force that she understood. We all do the best we can."

"June," April warns, "you cannot get mixed up in this. I don't have a good feelin.'"

"Too late," June says. "That choice was made a long time ago. In my church, just like a lot of things in life, what goes around comes around. The police will add Maxine's murder to their statistics, but in the end, this business will be settled outside the law."

"What do you mean, outside the law?" April voices.

June takes a last gulp of coffee and sets down the empty cup. She stands to leave. "Juju has its own form of justice."

CHAPTER 33

The Coop is empty. Daytime patrons sit quietly in the corner, smoking weed. The double doors open and Clyde drags Mama Moo inside. She is older but still ageless, agile, and strong. Mama Moo surveys the joint. It's not clear if she's proud or ashamed.

"Take me to my son," she snarls.

Clyde does her bidding.

Inside Mister's office, Mama Moo looks from Lucy to Mister without a word. She scans the voodoo altar, African masks, and lighted bar without reaction. Her son paces back and forth, flexing his metal prosthetic hand nervously, at both Mama Moo's scrutiny and his ailing girlfriend.

Lucy lies on the couch, covered in blankets. She is pale, delirious, and drenched with sweat.

"Mama, you have to help her," Mister pleads.

Mama Moo stares at her son for a long minute. "What did you do?"

Mister recoils like a scolded child. "She had a fix on her. I don't know whose. I fed her a rosewater elixir like you showed me. But it didn't help."

Mama cocks her head at Lucy, who moans with a delusion that only she can see. "Did you charge the elixir with the full moon?"

Mister nods. Mama Moo approaches the girl and slaps her awake. Lucy's eyelids flutter and open.

"Stick out your tongue, girl," Mama Moo demands.

Lucy looks at Mama Moo for a few seconds. She is delirious.

"Do it, Lucy," Mister instructs.

Lucy obeys. Mama Moo inspects her tongue, which is covered in a white crust.

"It's a fix, all right," Mama Moo notes. She turns to Mister. "Who'd you mess with?"

Mister shrugs and wanders over to his altar. "Plenty of people. What do they have to do with Lucy?"

"They're after her to get to you." Mama Moo wanders over to her son.

"It's probably the white witch," Mister mutters.

Mama Moo lays a hand on his shoulder. For a moment, Mister's face softens under his mother's touch. Within an instant, however, any notions of motherly love are dispelled when Mama Moo spits on his shoes in disdain.

"You never understood, did you?" Mama Moo says. "That girl is not like you. She only peddles light magic."

Mama Moo heads for the office door and turns back. "You are too stupid to help. I'm going home."

Mister's face reddens with rage. Without a word, he nods to Clyde, who takes hold of the old woman. "I don't think so, Mama."

CHAPTER 34

Pearl bustles through tourists and vendors on the street in front of her restaurant. She calls after June and April, who are window shopping after breakfast. "Miss June! Wait your tiny ass a minute, let me catch up."

June removes oversized sunglasses and smiles warmly at Pearl who approaches, panting with the exertion.

"The jungle drums told me this is your sister, April," Pearl says.

April nods her head but doesn't return Pearl's smile.

Turning her attention to June, Pearl says, "I wanted to let you know Maxine's family is sending her back to Georgia. Police have been at the restaurant every day."

"Sorry things ended up like this." June puts a hand on Pearl's shoulder. "But thanks for helping her with the job. Maxine really needed it. I know it was a favor to me."

"Shoot," Pearl says. "That ole' judge was the cause of Maxine's Abraham getting in trouble. So, I had a foot in that pile of shit too."

"The judge?" April asks.

"Judge Royale," Pearl answers. "My good-for-nothin' ex-husband."

"Soon-to-be ex-husband," June adds.

"Not soon enough," Pearl scoffs. "Word on the street is Mister's comin' after you next."

"Mister?" April shades her eyes with a hand.

June turns toward her sister. "Remember Mister? The son of the swamp witch? Friends with Billy way back?"

April's eyes stare into the distance. "Haven't thought about him in years."

Pearl dabs her forehead with a handkerchief. "Seems Mister doesn't like competition of any kind. Plus, he thinks you fixed his woman, Lucy."

"Fixed?" April fans herself with her hand.

"Cursed," Pearl explains. "April, you're standing in the presence of one of the highest voodoo priestesses in the South. Your sister is downright famous around these parts."

"Infamous, maybe," April counters.

June cuts off the conversation. "Thanks for the warning, but I'm leaving town for a while to let things cool off. Unless he's got a third eye, I'll be just fine."

"We'll catch up at Violletta's wedding this weekend," Pearl says.

"Oh shit," June exclaims. "I forgot. I'm not sure I can—"

Pearl cuts her off and turns to April. "I've renovated an old estate left to me by my grandparents. We're having a big shay-shay, makin' curry goat, lots a singin' and dancin'. I never had any kids, so I've adopted Violletta as my own. Anyway, it'll be good for all of us to have a break from all the trouble. April, please get your workaholic sister to put down her magic wand for a few days and come on out, will ya'?"

"I have time," April responds. "We'll come."

June looks from April to Pearl in astonishment.

"Well," June says with a smile. "Wonders never cease."

CHAPTER 35

June straightens her headwrap in the reflection of a dress shop window.

"Catholics have their habits," April says. "The Buddhists wear the orange robes. What kind of religion requires dressing like a clown?"

In response to April's attempt at humor, June struts about, showing off her outfit. "Ouch! That stings, because I believe I'm looking pretty damn gorgeous! I'll be happy to share anything in my closet. Knock yourself out."

Suddenly serious again, April looks at herself in the window, still wearing the same baggy housedress in which she arrived. "Now, why would I wish to look more foolish than I already do?"

"For fun, April. Fun!" June squeals and twirls around in front of the window. "When's the last time you had any fun?" June grabs April's arm and pulls her toward the entrance to the dress shop. April digs in her heels.

"No!"

"Yes!" June counters. "You've been wearing this one outfit over and over. Surely in all that luggage, you can find something else?"

"Everything in those suitcases is for you."

"What do you mean?" June asks.

"I'll show you later," April says.

Inside the dress shop, April vetoes every dress that June presents. June finally grabs a sexy red dress in April's size and hands it to her.

April shakes her head no.

"Yes!" June insists and takes the dress to the counter to pay. "Gotta have somethin' to wear to the wedding, right?"

*   *   *

Surrounded by loads of shopping bags, April tries on shoes in a cute boutique. June hands her another pair.

"Stop! Enough," April says. "I want a praline."

"C'mon, please?" June begs. "I'm jealous. Really, you can wear any kind of shoes you want. Try another pair, please."

April picks out a pair of red high heels and compares the color to her new dress, still in the bag. "Billy tells me no matter how much weight I gain, my feet stay beautiful. My husband gets turned on by my feet, of all things."

June surveys her own built-up shoe with sadness. April doesn't notice.

"What does Billy say about his wife bein' here?" June inquires.

April scoffs. "That salty dog doesn't know where I am. He was out fishing when I left the kids with his mama. I left a note on the refrigerator sayin' God told me to journey for forty days and forty nights. Religion has its perks. My goodness, God's told me all sorts of things over the years. Even Billy doesn't challenge the 'Big Guy.'"

June laughs. "Why, hullabaloo and tigers too, even preacher's wives have their juju! We're in real trouble now!" The sisters cackle with laughter.

CHAPTER 36

June and April maneuver their packages through the busy streets. A musician carrying a large case slams into April, sending her packages flying. The sisters scramble to recover their purchases from the sidewalk.

A young, tattooed man exits the nearby Rose Tattoo shop, carrying a pastry box. "Hey Miss June, need some help?"

"Hey, Charlie!" June says. "Yes, thanks."

Charlie helps the women retrieve their packages.

June gestures to April. "This is my sister, April."

Charlie looks confused, but friendly. "You've never mentioned family. I didn't think you had any. Hey, April, nice to meet you."

April shoots her sister a derisive look. "Nice to meet you too, Charlie. It's real easy to forget her river-bottom bunch, and it ain't easy to remember six nieces and nephews' birthdays . . . hell, names even!"

Charlie looks awkwardly at June and passes her the pastry

box he's been holding. "These are from Ruthy. A 'thank-you' of sorts."

June opens the box. Inside there are four beautifully decorated cupcakes.

Charlie addresses April. "Thanks to your sister, I'm celebrating my fifth wedding anniversary."

"She remembered your anniversary?" April scoffs. "Let me shake your hand." April holds out her hand, and June plops the cupcake box into it.

"Here, sis," June says coldly. "I'm sure you're just hungry." June turns to Charlie. "She gets mean when she's hungry."

April huffs at June.

Charlie discreetly pulls an envelope from his pocket and hands it to June. "Changin' the subject, but I clearly need to make new friends. They all knew exactly where The Coop was. A map is in the envelope." Charlie looks at his watch. "I'm late for my own anniversary. Gotta go."

"Thanks, Charlie." June waves goodbye. She turns to see April about to take a bite of one of the cupcakes. June slaps it out of April's hand so hard, it hits a nearby tourist in the head. June fights laughter as the tourist grumbles and wipes frosting from his shirt. "Sorry! So sorry!" she calls after him.

"What in the world?" April exclaims. "Even Bully Billy doesn't knock the food out of my mouth!"

"Charlie's wife Ruthy is a bad cook. I'll explain later," June says. June grabs the box of cupcakes and throws the entire thing in the trash.

CHAPTER 37

Inside the walk-in closet, June pulls Charlie's envelope from her purse and removes five crisp hundred-dollar bills. She deposits the money and the map to The Coop into her safe, which is filled with cash.

June exits the closet. April closes a window blind, shutting out the darkening night sky. She wanders over to June's bookshelf. Her fingers trail along the spines of June's collection of psychic, new age, voodoo, crystal, and similar titles. April stops on a bright yellow book and pulls it out. The pages inside depict drawings of voodoo ceremonies and sketches of herbs and animal bones. As she flips through the pages, an old, printed photo falls to the floor. She retrieves the black-and-white photo and studies it. A middle-school-aged April and elementary-school-aged June stand on the riverbank holding hands with their Louisiana Creole father and a young Alma Mae. June clearly favors her father's dark good looks, while April is the spitting image of her pale, plump mother.

"Well, for heaven's sake," April exclaims. "Look what I found."

June takes the photo in hand. "Wow. We don't even look related."

"You took after Dad in more ways than one, Sister," April notes.

"Yeah, and you"—June grabs the photo and stuffs it back into the book—"took after Mom. Stop snooping!"

*   *   *

Later that night, April bathes in June's oversized tub while sipping tea. She reviews her pile of new clothes on the bed. Against her better instinct, she smiles at the purchases. "Thanks for all the new duds, June."

"No problem," June says. She hobbles unevenly out of the closet wearing a silk robe and brushes her long, dark hair. "It's worth any amount to see you out of that housedress."

April smiles. She looks at the tub in which she soaks like a queen. "Where'd you get this monstrosity anyway?" she asks.

"It was a gift from Jay."

"Yuck!" April responds. "That just plain gives me the hee-bie-jeebies. I'm getting out right now!"

"Oh stop," June scolds. "Jay is a house painter. He rescued the tub from a renovation. It came from a mansion, my dear. Your ass is sittin' in a rich man's tub!"

"So, what was with the cupcakes?" April asks, changing the subject.

"Well, Charlie's wife is dyslexic," June says. "She means well but reads recipes backwards and practices good luck potions in her cooking. They're always wrong and usually make people sick."

"Good Lord."

A knock at the door sends April underwater. June scrambles to slip on a pair of her built-up shoes. She opens the door to find Jay dressed in a cheap Western-style pink shirt. He pulls June out into the hallway, aggressively kisses her, and tugs on her hair. He whispers in her ear, "When's the heifer leavin'?"

June gently closes the apartment door behind her. "Cut it out, Jay. I told you, I don't know when she's leaving, and it's none of your business."

Jay sighs in frustration. "You're no fun anymore. I'm heading to a party you don't want to miss. Get dressed. Come with me."

June shakes her head. "I thought you were supposed to be working tonight."

"I am working. I have a lead on a guy to fund my new bar."

June rolls her eyes.

"You'll see," Jay counters. "One day I'm gonna work for myself serving watered-down drinks to dumb tourists." He turns to leave.

"Meet you later in the courtyard?" June asks.

Jay nods and holds out a hand. "You got any cash? I might need a cab home."

June pulls a twenty from her robe pocket and hands it to Jay. He saunters away, whistling.

Back in the apartment, June slips off her shoes. April stands with wet hair in front of the mirror, holding her new red dress up to her shoulders.

"Red is the color of passion. It suits you," June says and plops on the bed.

April stuffs the dress back into the bag. "I can't possibly wear somethin' like that. What would people say?"

June sighs. "When you've lived with misunderstanding as long as I have, you learn it doesn't kill you. Besides, you don't know anybody in New Orleans." She hands the dress back to April. And April hands it back to her.

"June, you live in a big, colorful, peacock-feathered world. You always have. My world is small, maybe boring, but it's safe and decent."

June's face goes dark. "Do you really think you're so much better than me? A tiny life filled with routine and mundane chores?"

April dries her hair with a towel. "No matter how many bloody noses you got, you would always stand up to the bullies, defend the cripples, and bandage the wounded. I don't get it. Now you've become the attacker?"

June grabs a bunch of colored beaded necklaces and walks out onto the front balcony. She tosses the beads to passing tourists, who revel in the treasure. As June continues sprinkling beads down to the sidewalk, April joins her wearing the red dress.

"Was it only money?" April asks.

"What?" June answers. She is stunned to see April in the dress. "Wow, that looks amazing."

April ignores the compliment. "In the envelope from that graffiti junkie, was it only cash?"

"Please," June says. "His name is Charlie. And some people call that body art. Yes, there was cash."

April claps with faux enthusiasm. "All this witchcraft shit is about the money! Now, I can understand that! Why not? I've kissed a fair amount of Baptist ass before passing the collection plate myself."

"It's more complicated than that," June says. "Charlie's wife, Ruthy, was forever cheating on him. I gave him some advice, and I guess it worked. The money is simply a token of his appreciation and an exchange of energy. Of course, Ruthy hates me, so you can see why I didn't trust the cupcakes."

"Poison?" April asks.

"In the world of hoodoo," June answers, "you watch food very carefully. A lot of spells happen with food. That's why I eat at Pearl's. It's always safe."

"So, what advice do you give cheaters?" April asks. "Not that I know any, of course."

"Of course," June affirms. "Wait 'til the cheater sleeps and scrape dry skin from their heels. Bury it under the front doorsteps. It keeps them close to home."

April cracks up. "You're kiddin'! People actually pay you for that crock o' shit? What a racket! Money, money, money!" April jumps around laughing so hard she looks possessed.

"Cut it out, April! You're acting crazy."

"Unbelievable," April says. "You've actually gotten rich pedaling folk medicine and superstition. You gotta love it. No husband, no kids, but you've got money. I guess it would be unbearable growin' old without money."

June stiffens. "I've survived all these years by thinking I make a small difference in the world by helping people."

April realizes she's crossed the line. "Well, I mean, the reality is what it is, right?"

"Funny, dear sister, how I've always been able to count on finding salvation for my actions in your eyes," June says sourly.

"If you mean I've had to cover for your insanity most of my life, well, hell yeah," April says. "In school, church, I made stuff up. Like, 'Oh well, June's practicing for a play.' Or, 'She's writing a book.' Anything to cover up your stupid ideas. Who in the hell sees the world like you do? Do the rest of us a favor; keep your thoughts and feelings to yourself, 'cause newsflash, honey, people think you're downright delusional."

June tosses the remaining beads to passersby on the street. One of the girls lifts her shirt, exposing a red bra. June throws her a kiss. She turns to April. "For all my faults, at least I ventured to make things better, unlike you, sitting on your cushion of complacency. Hiding, always hiding! Hell, even to come and see me, it's taken you *years* to leave the parish you were born in. No curiosity, no imagination. For Christ's sake, April, how about a little original thought for a change?"

"How dare you!" April cries. She slaps June across the face.

June holds her cheek. She is transported to the old farmhouse, to the chastising of youth. Tears spring to her eyes.

April doesn't back off. "It's vulgar to minimize my life while we both know you're an imposter. How ridiculous, playing at being somethin' special just to get rich. Well, shame on *you* for taking advantage of weak people. Shame on you!"

June wipes her eyes on the sleeve of her silk robe. "Certainly, the Baptists have never done such a thing," June replies. "I'm going to bed."

As June steps back over the threshold, she is immediately unable to see. A black film covers her entirely. She turns to see April also encompassed by the black swarm. Both women scream and wave their arms, running back inside. The swarm of black flies envelops them.

June turns white and runs clunkily toward the bathroom, with April close behind her. The flies pour in through the open balcony doors by the hundreds. Both sisters attempt to shield themselves from the buzzing beasts.

As April screams, she sucks a fly down her throat. Jumping up and down hysterically, she coughs and gags.

June tears apart the bathroom cabinets, looking for something. She pulls out a bottle filled with purple liquid and sprays the air maniacally with purple mist. Instantly, the flies freeze in midair and dissolve. They are gone. April and June step tentatively back into the living room but see no more insects. They quickly shut both balcony doors and collapse onto the bed.

"What the hell, June?" April pants.

"A message from an old friend," June says.

"Friend?"

"The old witch down by the river," June replies.

April's eyes widen in recognition. "The mamaloi?"

June nods. "I think Mama Moo is calling me."

CHAPTER 38

In the silence of the night, June dresses while April sleeps. June dons black ninja gear and pulls her hair into a high ponytail. She retrieves the map to The Coop from the safe and sticks it into her pocket.

Before she departs, June is distracted by giggling sounds from outside. June creeps quietly onto the balcony and looks down into the moonlit courtyard. Jay sketches a nude model who lounges on a bench near the stone fountain. She holds a bottle of champagne and two glasses. Jay, fully dressed, walks to a nearby table and grabs a handful of Mardi Gras beads. He catches a glimpse of June on the balcony. Their eyes engage for a long moment.

Deliberately, Jay drapes the beads over the model's head and kisses her seductively. The young woman responds. For June's viewing pleasure, Jay holds the champagne glass high as a toast to June, then slowly pours the champagne on the woman's skin and eagerly licks it from her breasts.

On the balcony, June's stoic face reflects detachment and anger.

CHAPTER 39

June reviews the map and makes her way through the underbrush. Her black apparel blends seamlessly with the jagged branches and murky undergrowth of the river bottom. She stops at a small clearing through which she peers at Mister's establishment, The Coop.

June circles the building to see the dimly lit double-door entrance. June stops in her tracks. She is shocked to see Mama Moo. The old woman sits near the entrance and hovers over a bonfire, looking weak and tethered like a dog on a chain.

A barrel-chested armed guard watches over the entrance, perched on a stool by the double doors. He holds a sawed-off shotgun in his lap. June can see that Mama Moo's ankle bleeds from an iron claw and chain, which binds it to a spicket attached to the building.

Beside Mama Moo sits a makeshift altar that hosts a plate of food, a Virgin Mary statue, various colored candles, and a jar of money. There is a large basket of dried chicken claws next to her. As a stream of patrons enter The Coop, they snake past Mama Moo. She hands each of them a chicken claw, and they drop money into the jar, hoping for good luck.

"*Bonne chance*," she says quietly. "Good luck . . . *Bonne chance*."

As June watches from the shadows, Mister steps through the double doors. He hands Mama Moo a steaming cup of tea.

"You almost forgot your tea tonight, Mama," Mister says with a sinister grin.

Mama Moo merely hisses at her son.

"Now, c'mon, Mama. You know it's for your own good."

Mama Moo stares back at him defiantly for a moment, but then relents. She drinks the "tea" in one gulp and throws the cup into the fire, cackling loudly.

June rounds the corner of the long low building and peers into a dusty back window. Before she can get a good look, a vicious bark startles her. She drops for cover into the bushes. From her hiding place, she sees a bald armed guard patrolling the perimeter. He holds the leash of a pit bull, who clearly wants to take the lead.

"Who 'der?" the guard shouts.

June holds her breath. The dog pulls wildly at the leash. June has only seconds before she is discovered. The pit bull nearly chokes itself as the huge man squints into the darkness. "Is there someone out there?"

Just before he steps further into the underbrush, a skunk scuttles near the dog. The pit bull loses focus on June's scent and instantly chases the skunk.

"Oh shit!" the guard yells, smelling the skunk's signature

scent. He takes off running in the opposite direction of the stink, dragging the dog behind him.

Sensing an opportunity, June creeps back up to the dirty window. Inside, she sees patrons betting on a cockfight in one corner, while others sit at casino tables and watch the exotic dancers. Rowdy onlookers drink joy juice from mason jars and exchange bets. Beautiful young men and women pull patrons into back rooms.

June continues to work her way down the building toward the entrance. Although she stays hidden behind tall grass, Mama Moo instantly spots her in the darkness. June reaches into her black bag and pulls out a pair of wire cutters.

Mama Moo quickly shakes her head no, indicating the guard on the stool, unseen by June.

A silver luxury sedans screeches to a stop in the gravel, then idles in front of the building. June is distracted from the vehicle's arrival by the forceful opening of the double doors. Backlit as if on stage, Mister and Clyde exit the building. Mister opens the car door and welcomes Judge Royale.

As the two men shake hands and head back in, June and Mama Moo exchange a knowing look. Bad juju is about to happen.

CHAPTER 40

Inside The Coop, Mister and the judge sit in high-backed chairs in a dark corner. Mister smoothly pulls a cigar from his pocket with his prosthetic hand and gives it to Judge Royale.

Surveying the room, Judge Royale nods in appreciation and clips the end of the cigar. Mister lights it and surveys the crowded building.

"Things are good, eh?" Mister pulls a stuffed envelope from his pocket and hands it to the judge.

The judge weighs the envelope in his hand. "This feels about twenty percent lighter than last month." He takes a long drag on his cigar and blows the smoke in Mister's face.

Mister tries not to choke. It's apparent he defers to the judge within reason, but there is defiance in Mister's eyes. He retrieves a small glass vial filled with translucent white dust from his pocket.

"The dust is a fuckin' mother load," Mister says. "Do you know what it's worth?"

"A thousand an ounce," Judge Royale answers quickly.

"You think too small," Mister says. "This is power. The power to defeat our enemies. And now I know exactly who they are." Mister nods to the envelope in Judge Royale's hand. "I've made us both very rich, so don't get your panties twisted. Just get me more dust."

"Yeah, well," Judge Royale counters, "that honey hole will come to an end if Pearl gets the estate in the divorce."

"And what about our other problem?" Mister asks.

"Your boy is being taken care of," Judge Royale replies.

"I told you not to use Abraham," Mister scolds. "He knows too much about our operation. And now he's in jail where the cops can work on him."

The judge shakes his head. "Stop wasting time worrying. It's being handled."

CHAPTER 41

Outside the building, a break in action has left Mama Moo and June alone. When the front-door guard sneaks behind the building for a cigarette, June rushes to Mama Moo's side. Using all her strength, she strains to clip the heavy chains from Mama Moo's leg.

"A dove flies to me when I need a hawk." Mama Moo sighs.

"I got your message. I wanted to find out what I was up against," says June, "but I never expected to find you in chains."

"Mister won't let me go. I couldn't help his woman. She was too far gone. He didn't forgive me."

Knowing she's running out of time, June presses all her body weight on the wire cutters. Finally, she hears a snap and breaks the chain. She smiles with triumph. Mama Moo wails in pain and relief, causing the guard to peek around the corner.

Just in time, June ducks out of sight. Mama Moo waves him off and quickly ties a scarf around her bloody ankle. The guard goes back to smoking, unaware of the caper.

As he turns away, June helps Mama Moo sneak down the side of the building. She limps in pain.

"What's happened to you?" June asks.

"My power's been stolen," Mama Moo responds. "Mister's been working on me."

June leads Mama Moo further out of sight into the dark underbrush. "You once told me our power cannot be stolen, it's just disguised as something else."

Mama Moo trips but is caught by June.

*　　*　　*

At the front of the building, two drunken men wrestle onto the hood of the judge's car, setting off the alarm. Within seconds, the bald armed guard and his pit bull appear. They stop the fight, but the commotion has caused a large group to spill from the building, including Mister and Judge Royale.

Judge Royale pats Mister on the back condescendingly. "VIP parking? I'm lucky I still have tires."

As the judge drives away, Mister turns to face the building and freezes. He stares at Mama Moo's empty stool and broken chains.

With one flick of his prosthetic arm, the snarling pit bull appears at Mister's side, the bald guard in tow. Mister points to the basket of chicken claws, and the dog sniffs vigorously. The guard releases the dog into the woods. Mister nods silent instructions to go after Mama Moo and heads back inside.

CHAPTER 42

Mama Moo and June struggle to move through the thick underbrush as vicious barks grow closer. June turns to see a flashlight bouncing in the dark. She grabs Mama Moo's hand. "This way. I know a shortcut. The guard is right behind us."

"We're not going the same direction," Mama Moo says, resisting June's pull.

"I don't understand," June whispers. "Mister will come after us. I'll protect you, but you've got to help me manage his madness. I don't know how to get out of this mess without your juju."

"Our paths have always been divided," Mama Moo says. "You've chosen your rut. Only your own magic will find a way out. I'm goin' back home to the parish."

Mama Moo starts off on her own in the opposite direction. June is flabbergasted.

Out of nowhere, the tracking pit bull jumps from the darkness and knocks June over with a thud. The heavy beast pins June to the ground. June shields her face as her black leather jacket is torn to bits by the dog's thrashing teeth.

Mama Moo starts down the path to her escape. She glances back at June, who still fights the snarling dog. June is close to defeat. Mama Moo ducks into the bushes. She breathes heavily with effort. Although the drugs have begun to wear off, she's still weak. She looks again at the empty path—her escape route back to home and back to freedom.

The bald armed guard approaches June and calls off the dog. "Heel!"

The dog jumps from June and retrieves a treat from his master. The menacing man hangs his gun on his shoulder and salivates over a shivering June.

With sinister delight, he pulls a machete from his belt sheath. Its razor-sharp blade glistens in the moonlight.

He poises the blade over June's head and raises it high, ready for a deadly strike. As he brings the heavy blade toward June's throat, she rolls out of the way just in time, but the machete lops off her ponytail.

Panicked, June scrambles to her feet. The gigantic man raises his machete once more for the execution. In a blinding second, Mama Moo jumps from a tree branch above his head and lands on his shoulders like a panther.

With a mystical surge of energy, she swiftly wrestles his arm into a position in front of his face. As the guard struggles, Mama Moo bites his ear and rips it off with her teeth. With unusual strength, Mama Moo directs the guard's arm to slice his own throat. They both crumble to the ground as the machete falls from his hand.

Nearly decapitated, the guard bleeds out quickly. His pit

bull stops barking upon discovering the severed ear of his master, which Mama Moo has spit to the ground. The old woman quiets the dog with one stern look. With the ear in its mouth, the dog retreats into the bushes.

Mama Moo, fire-eyed and animalistic, picks up the ponytail and hands it to June. June hyperventilates.

Mama Moo says, "No one can breathe for you, child. We are born alone, and we die alone." She nods to June's ponytail. "You're gonna need that to deal with this properly. Your hair holds all your memories." In an instant, Mama Moo disappears into the darkness.

CHAPTER 43

Back at the apartment, April tosses and turns and reaches for June. She sits up and realizes she's alone. She scans the small apartment. The bathroom and closet doors are open, and the small rooms are dark. April is baffled—where could she be? Perhaps down at the shop. Her sister seems to spend an inordinate amount of time making sure that place is secure. Unless she's doing something else down there? April's mind wanders, unbidden, to a vision of Jay and June humping on the counter.

Shaking the vision away, April lumbers groggily to the kitchen, looking for a snack. She scavenges the refrigerator in search of food, but all that greets her is a head of wilted lettuce and a moldy block of cheese.

Without much hope, she opens the freezer door in a last-ditch effort for something to eat and stops suddenly. Inside the frosty compartment she sees only one thing. Maxine's frozen hand reaches eerily toward her. Upon seeing the frozen red blood crystalized on the wrist, April gags.

She barely makes it to the back balcony in time to vomit over the railing.

On the patio below, Jay and the nude model wake instantly as they are covered in the gross, warm liquid. The model screams and runs inside.

Jay looks up, wipes the goo from his face, and yells, "You bitch! You did this on purpose!"

April wipes her mouth. She is astounded at her luck. "Where I'm from, we kill the runts of the litter," she yells down to Jay.

Jay's face reddens with fury. "Wait 'til Junebug gets back! She'll send your fat ass packing!"

April gets loud. "Oh, sugar, you might wanna try growth hormones on that tiny little dick of yours. Junebug says that little thing barely tickles! And when she finds out you are a cheating little bastard, you're gone, buddy!"

Jay shoots her a bird and exits the courtyard, muttering obscenities all the way inside.

Back in the darkened apartment, June falls inside the front door exhausted. June's jacket and shirt are shredded to pieces, and her brunette hair is chopped off irregularly in the back. June is shaken.

April runs to her sister. "June, are you okay?" she asks frantically. "What in the world happened to you?"

June points to the kitchen cabinet. "Get me the salt. Quick!" June slams the front door shut and locks it. She grabs the salt from April and pours it across the threshold.

"I'll put the kettle on," April says and heads back into the kitchen.

June is spastic. She sees the shadow of a man flitter

across the ceiling. She screams at the shadow, "Shut the fuck up!"

"I didn't say anythin'!" April says, confused.

"Not you," June mutters. She climbs into bed, shaking and feverish. April crawls in bed next to June and holds her sister close.

"I need you to talk to me," June says to her sister.

"Sure, June," April answers. "It's okay, nothing's feelin' real to me either. Why, my heart is poundin' so fast, it's gonna jump the track any minute."

"Why do you think Daddy spent all that time down by the river?" June asks. Anything to change the subject in her mind and the nearly successful murder attempt she just survived.

"With the swamp witch, you mean?" answers April.

June nods.

"I never really understood it," April says. "And Mama didn't either. She just knew he was gone all the time, for one vice or another."

"That explains why we are so exceptionally fucked up," June stutters. She shivers.

April wraps a heavy blanket around her sister. "Go to sleep," April instructs. "That's what I do when everything goes sour. We'll talk tomorrow, go on to sleep now."

April cuddles June and hums a gospel hymn as June drifts to sleep.

CHAPTER 44

The coastline rolls by beautifully before April and June as they cruise down the highway in a vintage pink convertible listening to classic rock. Despite her bruised and scratched face, June is dressed to match the car, in all pink. April sports a new floral wrap dress, as fresh as the sea air.

"I don't guess there's a rat's ass chance of getting any explanation about last night?" April asks her sister.

June sighs. "Let's give it a rest for today, huh?"

April flicks at June's new short brown hairdo. "Remember how Mama would sit in the front porch swing, brushin' the dickens out of our hair? 'A hundred strokes, little missies.' Then insist we clean up every last loose strand for fear the birds would use them in their nests."

June nods in recognition. "Because it'd cause headaches if a bird used your hair in its nest. Maybe that clarifies why Mama had so many headaches."

"Little sister, you were responsible for a few of those headaches," April says with a laugh.

June laughs. "Oh, I think Daddy had a hand in them too."

The wind whips April's hair into her face. She pulls a scarf from her purse and ties it under her chin.

April turns down the radio and surveys the blue and brown choppy water of the Gulf Coast.

"Remember how Daddy talked to you?" June asks. "'Piggly wiggly, get me some coffee? Bring my socks, piggly wiggly?'"

"That's better than 'gimpy' I guess," April replies. "I don't think that rotten old man used our real names in all those years."

"He was jokin'," June says.

Both sisters survey the coast in silence for a few miles.

April breaks the silence. "You never came back. Not even for Mama's funeral. Disgraceful."

June side-eyes her sister and shrugs. "Why would I go back to people that treated me so badly? I hate that pitiful place."

"Watch it," April warns. "That's my home. If you mean Daddy, well, it wasn't just you. I settled the score for both of us. Fixed him real good."

"What do you mean?" June looks nervously at her sister.

"Honey," April says, "you never mess with the cook."

June looks at April, who keeps a stern look on her face for a moment. Unable to continue the ruse, she cracks a wicked smile. They laugh in sisterhood.

CHAPTER 45

earl's country estate sprawls over the landscape with a dominance that cannot be ignored. The manor house boasts a huge columned double porch and stands atop a gently sloping hill. The driveway is lined with giant oak trees, and the property includes a park area, fishpond, and informal gardens. Near the gated entrance to the estate, an ancient cemetery is unseen from the main driveway, nestled away from the house and accessible only by a dirt road.

June stops short of the main parking area and veers quickly onto a dirt road that winds into lush terrain. The car bounces in the ruts and comes to a halt at the ancient cemetery. The crumbling lot is surrounded by a rickety fence that has been freshly painted bright white. The cemetery is embraced by a sprawling Southern magnolia tree, laced with white prayer ribbons. June takes off her shoes at the white gate, where April stops to inspect a makeshift altar, which displays rosaries, candles, voodoo dolls, and assorted artifacts.

June approaches the giant magnolia tree, alive with fluttering white ribbons—symbols of countless pilgrimages of faith. She takes a white ribbon from her pocket.

"This is the spirit tree," she says to April. "Some people believe that when they die, their spirit comes back to the tree to jump into the next world." She ties the ribbon on a low-hanging branch.

"What are you doing?" April shouts from the gate.

"Sending a prayer to Mama," June answers. June makes her way to a small, iron-gated section of the cemetery. The entire graveyard is covered in glittering white dust with an iridescent glow, very different from the heavy black dirt outside the cemetery. She turns to April, still standing near the altar. "This place is as sacred as the Wailing Wall. It's the only place in the world that this kind of dust exists," June explains. "Root workers nor scientists can explain the phenomenon. The dust is exported around the world where hoodoo is still vibrantly practiced. It's potent magic . . . all kinda stories about healings and cures. This location has been a heavily guarded secret over the years. Only a handful of practitioners know about it."

June grabs a handful of the sparkling white dust and deposits it into a pouch. She rubs a little between her fingers. The dust flares into luminous, iridescent color for a few seconds, then returns to white. "Legend has it that on the day slavery was abolished, the black dirt turned into this magical white dust you see today. Believers pay top dollar for tiny amounts. Unfortunately, the dust doesn't discriminate between good and evil. It can save lives, but can also cause illness and death."

April's eyes widen at the strange phenomenon. "Doesn't it ever run out?"

June shrugs. "Not on this plot. Folks here have been using it for a century, and it hasn't run out yet."

April bends down and grabs a pinch of white dust. She is delighted to see it spark to life between her fingers. "Does this have somethin' to do with what happened to you last night?"

June nods her head. "Yes. Mister is rich from this dust, and he's in cahoots with Pearl's soon-to-be ex-husband, the judge. He's trying to get this land in the divorce settlement."

"Lord," April says. "I haven't thought about the swamp witch's son in years."

Exiting the cemetery, June grabs April by the shoulders. Her demeanor is grave. "Look, April, no matter what comes up this weekend, you do exactly as I say. *Exactly*. Do you understand?" Taken aback, April obediently nods.

CHAPTER 46

Pulling up to the front of the estate house, June and April see flowers, tents, and food vendors scrambling from front to back. April is visibly impressed with the magnitude of the estate house and what appears to be a very fancy affair.

Pearl bounds down the pillar-columned veranda to greet the sisters. "Hello, my lovely guests! I am happier than ants at a picnic that you both could make it!"

A gust of wind blows Pearl's straw hat from her head, as a second gust twirls June around. A brown pelican flies overhead and drops a load on April.

"Old Haitian saying," Pearl says with a smile, "Ye who gets dinky-dinked at a wedding is a mighty lucky lady."

June laughs. "Don't you feel lucky?"

"So sorry, April," Pearl gestures toward the house. "Let's get you cleaned up."

Cleaning herself off with a tissue, April responds, "'Answer a fool according to his folly.' Proverbs, twenty-six five."

As the ladies enter the grand hallway, the wind slams the front door shut behind them.

"Sure hope this wedding can beat the storm this weekend," Pearl laments. "They're sayin' it might turn into a full-blown hurricane."

"Don't worry," June comforts, "Violletta has the great skill of knowing how to guide her luck, even while waiting on it to show up. Her wedding will be lovely."

Pearl grins. "You have a way of makin' a person feel better. Thanks, June." Pearl gestures to June. "April, I give you credit. I didn't think anyone could get this workhorse to take a weekend off." Pearl turns to June. "Where's Jay?"

April snickers. "You mean, her dime-store cowboy?"

"Stop April," June warns. She turns to Pearl. "He had to work."

April scoffs. "Work, my foot."

"The mere mention of Jay's name is like barbed wire in her boot," June says to Pearl.

April gawks at the majestic interior, reminiscent of an era long gone. "Pearl, you have a lovely home. I had no idea what a treat I was in for this weekend."

April approaches a tapestry hung on a nearby wall. Its complex weaving depicts an orchard heavy with apples. "Wow, this is gorgeous."

Pearl beams. "My great-grandmother was a weaver. She and her sisters made several of these tapestries. They hang all over the city. There's even one in the governor's mansion."

June starts up the dual marble staircase, carefully holding onto the railing with one hand to help balance her ascent.

"C'mon, ladies," Pearl says. "Let's get y'all settled. Violletta is picking up her groom-to-be. They'll join us for the barbecue later."

Pearl sees a red cooler at the base of the stairs. "Does this go with you?"

"Oops." June halts and turns back. "This goes to the freezer, Pearl. We'll need it later."

Pearl nods in understanding.

CHAPTER 47

In the backyard, a huge bonfire is the center of attention as it spits sparks high into the twilight sky. A pig and a goat roast on skewers. Servers scurry about, offering drinks to guests. An aproned chef prepares a seafood boil at an outdoor kitchen. Jazz musicians serenade the sunset from under a large tree dripping with Spanish moss.

On the back veranda, June and Pearl review the festivities from rocking chairs. Violletta and her fiancé, Trent, saunter by and wave hello. Hand-in-hand, the happy couple walks off toward the yard's activities.

"Trent is a real sweetheart," June remarks.

"Yeah." Pearl sighs. "They're just so young. Hard to let go."

"It's quite the party, Pearl. You got room for all these people?"

Pearl surveys the expansive estate. "Yep. That's the beauty of this place. It holds a lot of ass."

They chuckle in a moment of friendship.

June shakes a set of keys at Pearl. "I was going to wait until the wedding tomorrow, but I'll go ahead and deliver these now."

Pearl inspects the keyring carefully. It's a miniature hand stamped with a third eye and the store name, "Miss June's Bizarre Bazaar."

"Does Violletta know you bought my shop for her?" June inquires. She tries to hide the bittersweet emotions that bubble up when she thinks about selling the shop to Pearl.

"No idea. It's going to be my wedding gift to her and Trent," Pearl says. "I'll wrap the keys up real pretty."

"Well, you get a bonus," June tells her. "The property comes with a ghost. The building was once owned by Tennessee Williams."

"Is he still hanging around?"

June chuckles. "You bet. TW's the best roommate I ever had."

Pearl tucks the keys into her pocket and looks sympathetically at June. "Where will you go?"

"Good question," June answers. "One thing's guaranteed, I will be takin' Jay and myself on one of those leisurely cruises to figure out what comes next. For the first time in my wanderlust, I don't have a clue."

Pearl smiles. "I remember some advice my friend *Miss June* gave me a while back."

June smiles at the mention of her alias, *Miss June*.

Pearl continues, "When you're stuck in the muck, just start by taking a step outta the place you're in. Then another step. Pretty soon, you're in a different spot altogether. Besides, you always have a home with me."

"Thanks, Pearl," June says warmly. "I wonder what Miss

June's advice would be for someone who was neck deep in shit and couldn't even take the first step?"

"Well, now," Pearl says. "I suspect she'd say, 'Turn your head . . . it will change the view.'"

They laugh.

CHAPTER 48

April strolls toward a koi pond nestled near the wooded perimeter of the backyard. Pearl's Haitian brother, Peter, sits on an ornate iron bench watching the brightly colored white and orange fish. His white suit and Panama hat suggest a suave demeanor befitting an old-time movie star.

When April approaches, Peter slides to the side wordlessly. In an unusual spontaneous act, April eagerly joins him. She notices two empty wine bottles under the bench. Peter offers April his glass. Instead of a dainty sip, she downs the full glass in one gulp.

"Your sister's quite an anomaly in the voodoo community," Peter slurs.

"You assume I know what *anomaly* means," April responds.

Peter laughs and scoots closer to her, grinning. "Feisty. I like that."

"Yup," she says. "My sister's a rock star, alright, in 'hoodoo' land. That's what I hear, anyway."

Peter looks at the empty wineglass in his hand. "And my sister holds the keys to the magic dust."

"You believe in that stuff?"

Peter shrugs and grabs the last bottle of wine from under the bench. "I just want to write poetry."

"Well, I'm from the river bottoms where people barely get away with life, let alone anything beautiful like poetry." April shivers in the cool evening air.

Peter removes his jacket and drapes it over her shoulders.

"Where's your wife?" April asks, unabashed.

"Oh, please. No civilized woman would have an old bastard like me." Peter empties the remaining red wine into his glass. "My dedication is to my sister. Pearl's resolute that it's our responsibility to preserve our ancestral history. Everyone has a cross to bear."

"And this estate is Pearl's?" April inquires.

Peter nods. "I wonder what happens when crusaders like our sisters decide not to save the world?" He smiles. "I guess the question really becomes, 'How selfish can the rest of us be?' Italy, for me as an example, is a cover."

"A cover?" April asks.

"Oh, indeed," he says. "Countless raging debates about wasted capacities led me to sell my shares in the estate back to Pearl and bolt to the old country. My sister carries high-minded concepts about my being a Haitian man in a sordid world."

"A sordid world," April says thoughtfully. "A sordid world indeed."

As April keeps Peter from tipping over, he says, "You see, in her eyes—"

"Whose eyes?" April interrupts.

"Pearl's," he says. "In her eyes, I'm running from my duties, trying to get away with living instead of pursuing some grand, glorious purpose. I don't want to deal with saving the planet or the estate, for that matter. No matter how many slaves died with brick and mortar on their hands."

April nods in sympathy. "June has strong convictions too. Who has time for such frivolous thoughts?"

"I just want to write poetry." Peter sighs.

"And I'm from the river bottoms where we all just barely get away with life," April repeats.

"So," Peter says, "it's a plain arrangement?"

"Yes." April shrugs. "If you don't point out my lack of effort, then I will overlook your mediocrity! It works just fine."

Peter grins. "You assume I know what *mediocrity* means."

"I've never known anyone that actually *lived* in Italy," April says. "The only foreigners I really know are from the next county over."

"*Siete assolutamente delizioso* . . . You're so beautiful," Peter says in Italian, then English. "I'm there for a year. Don't wanna stay away from Pearl and Violletta much longer than that."

"My goodness," April says. "I'm sitting here dressed like a tomato, having a sophisticated conversation with a famous poet, and a good-lookin' one no less. That's plenty to send those foamin' tongues at my Sunday school class a-floppin' for the next ten years."

Peter laughs and grabs April up by the arms and pulls her close to him. April poises for a kiss, and Peter looks at her for a long moment.

"How about the not-so-famous poet would like to dance with a beautiful woman?" he says.

"No, sir," April replies. "I've never learned to cock my tail."

"Everyone can dance," Peter says. "C'mon."

Peter takes April by the hand, and they rise from the bench. He lightly places a hand on April's back and they twirl clumsily around the pond a few times. The pair ultimately plops back onto the bench. Peter lights a cigarette and hands the pack to April.

"I don't smoke," April says. After a beat, she snatches at the pack. "Gimme one." She takes the cigarette and chokes out a few puffs.

Peter cleverly blows smoke rings for April to mimic. She tries and half succeeds.

"You're not one of those tragic poets always glorifyin' the past, are you?" April asks Peter. "I mean, yesterday is gone, right? It's done, kaput, never gonna be changed."

"I like to write about the moments when things tasted and smelled better," Peter responds. "When life was all anticipation. A place where time never catches you."

"Oh, honey." April chuckles. "Forget about it. That sweet bird flew his coop. It's called youth."

They laugh.

CHAPTER 49

June stands as Pearl continues to rock. She stretches and looks down at the party in full swing. Violletta and Trent effortlessly glide across the dance floor, rehearsing for their first dance the next day. June points toward April and Peter, looking cozy by the koi pond. "How long is your brother staying?"

"Just 'til he walks our bride down the aisle," Pearl answers. "Then he's heading back to Italy. He sold me his shares in this place and never looked back."

"This place is so big," June says. "Will the kids move in with you?"

"I wanted to give them the deed to the back pasture so they could build a house, but my lawyer says to wait until the divorce is final." Pearl shrugs. "When I croak, she'll get the whole place anyway."

"But I hear our favorite Judge Royale is trying to get the whole damn place out from under you," June grumbles.

"Yeah, I can't imagine why," Pearl scoffs. "According to him, it was nothin' more than a money pit."

"We both know it's not the house he wants," June says. "It's the cemetery dust."

Rocking in her chair, Pearl takes a deep breath.

June knows she wants to say something. She takes her seat again. "Spit it out, Pearl."

"Just got word earlier today," whispers Pearl. "Abraham died in jail. They say he was poisoned."

June stifles a gasp with her hand. She feels a rush of adrenaline pump through her veins. Bending over to get a full breath, she sticks her head between her knees, trying to avoid a full-blown panic attack. A moment later, she raises her head. "That whole family . . . ruined."

Pearl pats her on the back. "Buck up, sister. No room for paper tigers. The war's not over yet."

Short of breath, June manages to squeak, "I can't breathe. I'm choking."

"On guilt and regret, maybe," Pearl says. "Let's get you to bed."

Pearl helps June to her feet and discreetly escorts her friend to her room.

*   *   *

The guest room, refined and stylish, is punctuated by a Juliet balcony that overlooks the festivities in the backyard. June lies on the bed with a washcloth on her forehead. Pearl opens the balcony's French doors for some fresh air and sits beside her friend. She picks up a family photo and shows it to June. Three preteens, circa 1994, hold a Haitian flag above their heads.

"You and Peter?" June asks, happy for the distraction.

Pearl nods proudly. "And Priscilla, our older sister. Violletta's mother." Pearl points to the middle girl, who is a head higher than the others. "Our father used to call us 'three peas in a pod.'"

"Pearl, Peter, Priscilla," June repeats. "Three Ps. Where's Priscilla now?"

Pearl sighs. "The night we left Haiti, there were only three seats in the raft. Not the six Daddy had paid for. Priscilla insisted I take baby Violletta. She stayed with Mama and Daddy. They promised they'd be on the next boat. Grandma was waiting for all of us in New Orleans. She'd married an American Marine years before."

"Really?" June asks.

"Florence was a real pistol. Back in the fifties, some Marines came to Haiti to help train up our soldiers. Grandpa Louis took one look at Grandma and grabbed her up." Pearl waves an arm around the room. "His family owned this place. They're both buried in the cemetery."

"So, Priscilla and your parents? They never got out?" June asks.

Pearl shakes her head sadly. "Peter and I searched for years, but we never found them." Shaking off the memory, Pearl gets up and pulls open the bottom drawer of the dresser. She hands a wrapped gift to June. "Happy belated birthday, Miss June."

June smiles. "I don't have birthdays anymore, remember? Thank you, Pearl."

"Yeah, well," Pearl says, stepping over the threshold to the balcony, "as your ghost would say, 'Time is the longest distance between two places.'"

"I never really knew what that line meant," June muses.

"Neither do I. Open your gift."

June tears off the gold wrapping paper and opens the box. She stares incredulously at its contents. "A Bible?"

Pearl nods as June pulls out a large, white leather-bound Bible with gold trimming.

"One of the greatest books ever written," Pearl says. "All the significant world movements in recent history were accomplished with the language from the Bible."

"A few wars too." June looks at her friend. "But you're an atheist?"

Pearl nods. "A very angry atheist at the moment."

June holds up the Bible. "Are you tryin' to be funny?"

Pearl sways with the dance music wafting up from the yard. The warm breeze tousles her hair. She speaks to the night. "I watched wretched things happen in Haiti, and I loathe the potions and spells handed out to the weak and vulnerable, when what they needed was medicine and food. And I hate that God-damn dust out there. But like every other spiritual practice, voodoo has helped people. To my own disbelief, I've seen it work."

June joins her on the balcony. "Sometimes a rational mind can't explain the unnamed mysteries of life."

"Well, I don't know about unnamed mysteries," Pearl replies. "But I've lived long enough to believe in helping people. So, if folks think that cemetery dust out there is their savior, then I'll protect their hope as long as I can. Now, open the Bible."

June flips open the garnished gold Bible and cackles in surprise.

CHAPTER 50

Violletta's elaborate wedding is in full swing. Peter walks his niece down the aisle, which follows a path from the dramatic front steps of the estate past the pink rose garden, ending at a lavish arch on the front lawn, decorated with wildflowers. Among a group of friends and family, Violletta and Trent jump the broom of marriage.

At the culminating moment, Trent kisses his bride, and guests cheer their congratulations. Peter and Pearl, the proud elders, hug each other in a true moment of joy.

*   *   *

The wedding reception booms food, music, and celebration. Guests enjoy the beautiful day, for the moment; however, the bright sunshine is threatened by dark clouds in the distance.

Under a massive white tent housing an elaborate buffet and a three-tiered wedding cake, June shoves a plate of food toward April.

April moans and pushes it away. "No thanks." She is clearly not feeling well. Her brow beads with sweat.

"Did you partake in too much swamp juice last night?" June teases.

April mops her brow with a napkin.

Peter floats up to the table and extends a hand to April. "I'm leaving soon; how about a final dance?" Peter says, eyes sparkling.

April smiles weakly at Peter but shakes her head. "Wish I could. Not feeling well."

Peter nods. "Well, you and June have an open invitation to Italy. Visit me anytime. I just wanted to say goodbye before I leave."

Peter and April share a smile. Within it, an alternate reality is known by both of them. What could have been. Another time, another place.

*   *   *

As the reception winds down for the evening, Violletta and Trent wave goodbye to their guests from a ribbon-decorated convertible. Guests blow bubbles at the happy couple and cheer them as they roll out of the driveway.

Violletta reaches for Pearl's hand. Pearl wipes a tear from her eye. "Y'all call me when you get to Baton Rouge," Pearl says.

Violletta nods. "I will. Aunt Pearl, thank you for everything."

Pearl smiles at her lovely niece. "You look like your mother in that dress."

With both women on the verge of tears, June pulls Pearl away from the car and puts an arm around her shoulder. They wave to the newlyweds as they drive off into the sunset.

CHAPTER 51

Tossing and turning in one of the guest beds, April can't sleep. She notices June's empty bed.

"June?" she calls out. No answer.

April lumbers out of bed and opens the French doors. She steps onto the breezy balcony to find a brooding sky. A storm is coming.

In the distant woods that skirt the estate, April sees a strange orange glow. She listens to the night. Behind the chirp of the cicadas, she hears a distant beat. It calls to her.

*   *   *

April worms her way through the underbrush toward the sound of drums and chants. She moves in the direction of the orange glow. It comes from an enormous bonfire. She approaches the clearing as flames eagerly lick the sky and cast a mesmerizing light over the old cemetery that she and June had visited upon arriving. April watches curiously from a safe distance.

Through the underbrush, she spots her sister, dressed in all white. June holds her own severed ponytail in the air. She dances around the bonfire like a Bohemian goddess. June meditates on her ponytail for a long moment, then releases it into the fire.

Pearl, on the sidelines but not participating, observes from a lawn chair. A dozen people snake around the fire in a trance, all wearing bright white clothing. The group of like-minded individuals—some of whom were at the wedding—practice the voodoo ritual with fervor. They chant along with the drums.

Stunned by the sight, April crosses herself like a Catholic, even though she's a good Baptist. Her hair is blown into her eyes as the wind picks up violently. Severe weather is imminent.

The white clothes of the practitioners flitter in the rising wind, and the tongues of the bright flame waver in the strong gusts. An elderly woman holds a live chicken by the neck. The bones crack as she twists the bird fiercely, breaking its neck. Immediately, a young, skinny man slices the chicken's neck with a sharp blade and passes the headless bird around the circle. A woman wearing a colorful head wrap tips the chicken's open neck to her lips and sips its blood.

From April's hidden spot, she watches as the head-wrapped woman passes the chicken along to the next dancer, who also sips blood. April gags at the sight and bends over to heave in the dirt.

June retrieves Maxine's severed hand from her cooler. She raises it above her head.

The group chants, "*Ouanga te papa Legba, Legba Touton, Legra Atibon Toute hounci fait croix*" in honor of the gatekeeper to the spirit world, Papa Legba.

June approaches Pearl and presents her with Maxine's severed hand. They exchange a knowing look, and Pearl nods to June, who turns and throws the hand into the fire. June then walks to the edge of the nearby cemetery, opens the white iron gate, and grabs a handful of the sparkling white dust.

As she does, the cemetery floor illuminates into translucent wonder, then fades back to white. In response to the disturbance, the giant spirit tree in the middle of the cemetery rustles its white ribbons. June acknowledges the tree, pulls a hair from her head, and drops it as an offering. Satisfied, the tree relaxes back into silence. June deposits the dust into a wooden bowl and returns to the bonfire. The sky rumbles with menace.

The practitioners fall silent. The only sounds are the crackling of the fire and the rising wind. June dips her finger into the bowl of dust and draws a cross on each practitioner's forehead.

She walks to Pearl and silently asks for permission. "For protection," June says. Pearl nods her consent. June anoints Pearl's forehead in white dust, and then herself.

Surprised by the sense of peace she feels, Pearl smiles at her friend. June turns toward the group of practitioners and bows to them—a gesture of thanks for their contributions to the ceremony. A sense of serenity envelops the scene.

CHAPTER 52

April has seen enough. She holds her stomach, still feeling nauseous and weak. Before she can make any headway back toward the house, April is startled by two speeding SUVs tearing up the road. The black missiles pass too close, and a side mirror clips her temple. April slumps to the ground.

The roaring vehicles skid to a halt near the bonfire. June gasps as Mister exits and slams the heavy door shut. Pearl jumps from her seat. Everyone around the fire freezes.

Wielding a machete, Mister's private security guard joins the fray. From the second SUV, Judge Royale, flanked by his own guard carrying an automatic weapon, exits the car. The spikey haired man sprays the air with bullets. Everyone screams and drops to the ground. Judge Royale makes a bee-line for Pearl.

Suddenly, an ear-splitting crack of thunder causes the guards to drop for cover. A second later, a blinding bolt of lightning illuminates the giant spirit tree in the nearby cemetery.

June sees Mama Moo wildly perched at the top of the tree. No one else seems to notice.

A second flash of lightning hits an above-ground tomb, sending electrical currents through the cemetery's white dust. The entire cemetery floor becomes an iridescent rainbow. Everyone is transfixed by the strange phenomenon.

Taking advantage of the distraction, the machete-wielding guard races to June, throttles her by the throat, and holds the razor-sharp blade against her neck. A trickle of blood stains her white shirt.

Judge Royale grabs Pearl by the arm and drags her closer to the fire. "Time to settle this, *mon oiseau doux*, my sweet bird," he whispers to his wife. He forces Pearl so close to the flames that her rubber-soled shoes begin to melt. "Don't worry, Pearl, I will take good care of your precious cemetery."

Pearl struggles to escape his grip and retreat from the flames. The judge pulls papers from his pocket and shoves them into Pearl's face. "Time to sign, bitch."

In a booming voice, June calls out, "In the name of the ancestors, leave her alone!"

Judge Royale sends a silent command to Mister, who nods to the guard with the machete. The thick-necked man shallowly slices the side of June's throat. June screams in shock and pain as a river of blood flows down her neck. Her white shirt is now soaked with red. June's eyes flutter, but she remains conscious, for the moment.

A crack of thunder sends a shock through the group. A brilliant flash of lightning illuminates Mama Moo perched at the top of the spirit tree. This time, *everyone* sees the old woman. The tree's white ribbons flow beneath her like an eerie wedding dress.

"Mister!" Mama Moo bellows in a voice unnaturally amplified. Mister jumps, startled, and meets his mother's gaze. He is shocked and confused by her presence.

"Not this time, Mama." Without hesitation, Mister rushes June, knocking the machete free from the guard's grip. Before anyone can react, Mister grabs the nearby weapon with his prosthetic hand.

June scrambles to escape, but too late. Mister grabs June's thin neck with his natural hand and squeezes. For a moment, June scratches and pulls at Mister's arm, but she quickly realizes it's no use—his strength is immense.

A few of the practitioners race to help June. Before they can come close, the bald guard shoots at their feet, stopping them short.

June's lungs burn. She feels her life force slipping away. Instantly, she is transported to that moment with Mama Moo under the water. She can still see the old woman's cold eyes, blurred as in a watercolor painting. June releases herself, abandoning her body to the fate before her. She goes entirely limp.

Mister raises the machete in his prosthetic hand high above his head—ready for the death blow.

"June!" screams Pearl. She starts toward June, but is held in place by her husband.

Mama Moo scrambles down the tree and moves quickly toward the bonfire. She grabs a handful of cemetery dust from the ground and blows it like a kiss toward Mister. "Flee like dirty angels out of the devil's mouth," Mama Moo screeches.

A bolt of lightning snakes to the ground from the menacing dark sky above. It strikes the tip of the raised machete clasped in Mister's prosthetic hand. The electrical current flows through the metal arm and knocks the machete to the ground. Mister collapses in a heap, electrocuted.

June is released. She crumbles. After a moment of stillness, her body wakes up. June sucks in huge gasps of sweet air.

Stunned by the events, Mister's guard drags his boss into the SUV and speeds away.

June jumps to her feet and applies pressure to her neck. A nearby practitioner hands her a scarf and the wooden bowl of dust. June hastily slathers the wound with dust and wraps her neck with the scarf. She runs toward Pearl.

The group, dazed at the quick succession of events, recover their wits. The crowd pushes murderously toward Judge Royale. He releases Pearl and runs for his life. Before he can escape into his SUV, a loud hiss draws his attention to Mama Moo in the cemetery. Mama Moo is illuminated strangely by swirling, glowing, translucent white cemetery dust. A tornado of magic envelops her.

Judge Royale is paralyzed with fear. He grabs his left arm and then his chest, and crumples to the ground. His guard has seen enough. He retreats into the SUV and speeds away, leaving the judge on his own.

Pearl runs to Judge Royale and begins CPR. "He's havin' another heart attack!" she yells. "Someone call 911!"

June sees April stagger toward the fire. "April! Are you okay? Sit down here and wait."

April takes a seat on one of the tree stumps that circle the fire. "I'm okay."

June rushes to Pearl's side. She tries and fails to find a pulse on the judge's neck. She shakes her head at Pearl. "He's gone."

June looks at the now-empty spirit tree within the cemetery. Mama Moo is nowhere to be seen. A massive thunderclap booms overhead, and heavy rain washes over the scene.

CHAPTER 53

June's pink convertible struggles against the weather. The opposite side of the highway is busy as people evacuate New Orleans to escape the impending tropical storm. Fierce winds whip June's car from side to side, and she clutches the wheel tightly to maintain control. April fitfully sleeps in the passenger seat as June fiddles with the vintage radio. A bandage on June's neck is the only evidence of the previous night's drama.

June finally lands on a scratchy station. "*Authorities have declared it official. Tropical storm warning . . . stay home . . . shelter in place . . . weather center has issued a—*" Finally, June loses the weak signal entirely, and the radio emits only static. She bangs on the dash and swerves to avoid a branch on the road. As they get closer to the city, more debris litters the road, sheets of driving rain obscure the highway, and trees bend in submission to high winds.

*   *   *

June rounds the corner to see deserted streets, closed and boarded-up businesses, and blinking streetlights. The Miss June's Bizarre Bazaar neon sign dangles precariously above the sidewalk.

June parks in front of the shop and nudges April hard on her shoulder. "April, c'mon. Let's get inside."

April jerks awake, and they both exit the car, awkwardly fighting strong winds and whipping debris.

Inside the building, June runs ahead of April and bangs on Jay's apartment door. April continues up the stairs toward June's third-floor flat.

"Jay!" June shouts. "Jay! Open up!"

"C'mon, June," April yells from the top of the stairs. "You've got the keys. Open the door up here."

June sighs in annoyance when Jay doesn't answer. She follows April up the stairs. June enters the apartment just as April grabs her side in pain. June barely notices and heads for the walk-in closet to change her clothes, which have gotten wet from the storm.

"April," June calls to her sister, "you should get out of your wet clothes first."

The lights blink on and off as April falls onto the bed in pain.

Suddenly, June screams from inside the closet. She drops to her knees to inspect an open, empty safe.

"What is it?" April asks from the bed with a moan.

Without answering, June grabs a set of keys in a box on the shelf and bolts from the closet and out of the apartment.

April clutches her pelvis and screams. She struggles to get up and falls back on the bed.

*   *   *

Downstairs in Jay's apartment, both sets of French doors are wide open. The wind whips them open and shut with loud bangs. June quickly secures the doors as the apartment lights blink on and off.

She turns to look at the space. It's completely empty. She stares at the only item left in the room—a life-size nude painting of herself. For a moment, she cannot breathe. Finally, she comes back to herself. The pit of her stomach is raw and she can't contain a stream of tears.

June's isolation is an abyss; she is tortured by betrayal. Although she knew, always knew, that Jay was a selfish prick, she believed somewhere down deep he loved her. Now, staring at the beautiful but invasive private image of herself, she realizes what she should have known all along. The only person Jay loves is himself.

It only takes a moment for June's sadness to curdle into anger. She runs to the empty kitchen, throws open the junk drawer and finds a pair of scissors. She crosses to the painting and slashes it into ribbons.

CHAPTER 54

An hour later, after June has spent all her anger, she returns to her apartment to find April. Her sister is still dressed from the waist up and sits in the bathtub full of water. April grips the sides of the tub and moans as blood reddens the bathwater around her.

"April!" June screams. Before she can reach her sister, the shadow of a man passes behind April. The lights blink off, plunging the room into darkness.

June fumbles for a candle. "April, are you okay?"

"I'm okay," April says shakily, as the room illuminates with the candle's dim glow.

June finds her phone and frantically dials 911. A busy signal emits, so she hangs up and tries again.

"Hang on, April," June reassures her sister. "All the circuits are out. I'm going for help."

"No . . . stop. Wait!" April shouts. "I need you to focus. Get some fresh towels."

"What?" June asks, bewildered.

April grimaces in pain and looks her sister in the eye. "We're having a baby."

*   *   *

The next morning, despite the violent storm that raged throughout the night, the sun shines brightly on the destroyed city.

In June's flat, sunshine streams through the French doors as June and April sleep on the edges of the bed. A newborn baby, wrapped in a towel, lies between them, also asleep.

June rises and opens the French doors. Her head throbs, her shoulders ache, and her hair is a wild, knotted mess. She looks at April, who, alternatively, sleeps peacefully and looks as normal as the day she arrived.

April stirs. "June?"

June runs to April's side. "You okay?" June asks her. "One of my clients has a daughter that is a doctor. I'm going to call her."

"Sure," April says, "but I've done this before. You did great. Get that red bag over there, would you?"

June retrieves one of April's many pieces of luggage and opens it to reveal baby clothes, formula, and bottles. Her face fills with realization. "You planned this?"

April nods. "What should her name be?" she asks as they both survey the baby with weary, but happy smiles.

June is flabbergasted. She considers the previous two nights and everything they'd been through. June was almost killed by a one-armed voodoo devil, she and her sister survived a dangerous tropical storm, and April gave birth. "April, I truly have no idea."

CHAPTER 55

June holds the wriggling, tiny infant as an African-American woman, Dr. Alata Lafayette, examines April on the bed.

"Looks like everyone's healthy," the doctor tells them. She pulls off latex gloves. "Good job, June."

June smiles with relief. "Doctor, thank you so much for coming. I know everything's a mess out there."

Dr. Lafayette nods. "My mother would never forgive me if I didn't help you. After all, she says you've helped her many times." She tosses the soiled gloves into the trash and begins buttoning up her medical bag. "What's the baby's name?" Dr. Lafayette asks, picking up her clipboard.

"Unknown," June answers. "April can't decide."

"Okay, what's the father's name?"

"Unknown," April says.

"Unknown?" June questions.

"Unknown," April repeats.

The doctor senses something uncomfortable and sticks

the clipboard into her bag. "Okay, when you're ready, let me know what you decide for the birth certificate."

June thanks the doctor and walks her to the door.

April carries the baby onto the back balcony and holds the baby high, like an offering to the sun. "Mama said if you allow the sun to shine into a newborn's mouth, it will ensure a sunny disposition."

June steps onto the balcony behind them. April turns and immediately hands the baby to June.

Snuggling the baby, June says to her sister, "You should have told me."

"Yeah," April answers. "Change of life, baby. It's always the same for me. Usually, no one can tell I'm pregnant. A shame, really, 'cause I don't get any of the usual courtesies."

"Billy didn't notice?" June asks.

"Oh, honey. We're married," April responds. "We never touch each other. Every couple of years, he relieves himself, and I get another baby. Do you realize how long I've had someone suckin' on my tit? I mean, what's the moral of that story?"

"Mama Moo would say, 'Choose your rut carefully,'" June tells her, cooing at the baby.

April shrugs. "So, all your money's gone?" April asks June.

"My life's gone."

"What about your bank accounts?" April presses.

"Minimal," June says. "Cash business, you know. The money from the sale of the shop was in the safe, too."

"A cash sale? That seems risky," April notes.

"The safe was bolted down, for Christ's sake!" June defends. "And fireproof!"

"Just not asshole-proof." April chuckles.

In June's arms, the baby squeals. June holds out the squirming infant to her sister, but April ignores the gesture and heads back to bed. June tries to comfort the baby.

*   *   *

That night, as the baby sleeps in a makeshift crib—a drawer in the dresser—a weary June sips tea. April stirs from a nap.

"Want some?" June says, offering tea.

April shakes her head no and points to her luggage. "You need to open the luggage now," she instructs.

"Don't speak to me like one of your children," June says, exhausted. "I'm too tired."

"Please," April pleads. "I brought them for you."

"I'm sick of fuckin' surprises," June says. "I just want to sit still for one minute. Shit, a person can die from too much drama, you know."

"Not when they enjoy it as much as you do," April tells her. "Just open them."

"Later," June says.

Light notes of jazz float in through the open French doors.

"Can't believe the buskers are back already," June says. "I thought the storm damage might keep the ole' French Quarter quiet."

April nods in agreement. "It's the best quality of New Orleans. Its resilience."

In response to a cry from the drawer, June gives the baby a bottle as April slowly emerges from bed. She steps through the open French doors and overlooks the street. Crews of city workers are out in force, piling branches and debris onto trucks.

June joins her sister on the balcony and perches the baby on her shoulder for a burp. Both sisters take a moment to survey the wind-damaged, flooded city streets.

"When Billy goes to sleep at night, he empties his change on the nightstand," April tells June. "Every morning while he's still snoring, I claim those coins for my own indulgence. I deposit them in a mason jar hidden in my pantry, and by the time my birthday rolls around every year, why, shoot a monkey, I've got a small fortune. I farm out whatever children are in the house, dress in my Sunday clothes, and take the bus to the Grande Hotel, you remember? The one that looks like a castle?"

After getting a good burp, June tries to hand the baby back to April.

April shakes her head no and continues. "I get a room overlooking the lake and I order the most expensive food on the room service menu. When it comes, I consume every morsel like it is my last supper. I then return home on the 4:15 bus just in time to fix a modest meal for my family."

June gives April a sympathetic but stunned look. "Don't beat yourself up, April. I'm a big believer in situational ethics. In fact, I'd say I've embraced that reasoning most of my life."

"Good thing," April tells her. "Since we all know you love to piss in the wind." They smile at each other. "Nine months ago," April muses, "on my birthday pilgrimage, the stakes became more intriguing when a gentleman sat down beside me on the bus. Now, in that moment, somethin' fantastic happened. We actually spoke to each other without pretense, with uncensored honesty and unedited dialogue. It seemed his car had broken down, and the gentleman was goin' to the hotel to meet a client."

June sniffs the baby's butt. "She needs a change."

April points to the kitchen. "Diaper bag's over there."

June huffs in frustration but collects the bag and begins to change the baby's diaper.

"So, what was his name, this guy on the bus?" June asks, rolling the dirty diaper into a ball and tossing it into the trash.

"We never spoke about names," April responded. "Instead, we connected in a way I had never experienced with another person. It seemed the gentleman enjoyed curvy women, you know, one of those chubby-chaser guys. Well, it was tragic, really. His wife had lost so much weight through illness that the poor soul couldn't get his dingy up anymore. Sad, he said, since he loved his wife very much."

"You're makin' this up," June accuses. She finishes snapping the onesie on the baby, now freshly changed, and tries again to hand her to April. Again, April walks away without looking at the child.

"That pisses me off," April scoffs. "You think I'm telling this story just to amuse you? That's messed up, June."

"I'm sorry," June apologizes. "Please go on."

April picks up where she left off. "I had never worn a bathing suit before that day. He said it was a birthday gift. He got it from the shop in the hotel. We swam in the lake and had a real fine day. The gentleman said all the right things. That skinny little man made this big woman feel wanted. All

I'm obliged to say further is, we used some of your 'situational ethics' and created a fantastic memory that turned into that sweet little thing you're holding."

June's eyes widen with shock, but not with judgment. She gazes at the baby girl in her arms.

CHAPTER 56

With April and the baby asleep, June sits in the middle of the floor, surrounded by April's luggage. All the suitcases are open and filled with wrapped gifts addressed to "Alma Mae" from "June Mae."

A stack of unopened letters lies on the floor near June, the seals and stamps indicating they were sent from different countries at different times. As with the packages, the letters are all addressed to June's mother, Alma Mae.

June weeps as she reads a letter, written in her own handwriting, "*Mama, you wouldn't believe the sights to see here in Italy. I wish you could breathe in the open air at the Colosseum, taste the wine on your lips, and get a wink from a handsome stranger. This entire place looks like a painting . . .*"

April wakes up and takes a seat next to June on the floor.

"I've never felt so twisted," June says. "Mama never opened one of these."

April scoffs. "It's always about you, isn't it? You killed Mama the day you left. We didn't even know where you were for the first year. She went to bed and never got up. Shame on you!"

"Shut up, April," June warns.

"No!" April responds. "Not on your life!"

June claps her hands over her ears and scoots away from her sister.

April picks up a package and throws it at June. "You always leave a mess for someone else to clean up."

"Shut up!" June shouts. She still holds her hands over her ears in a childish attempt to drown out April's words.

April throws another package at June. "I'm grateful, really I am. Really! You left me with no choices. Therefore, I have no regrets. Think about a life with no regrets! Aren't you jealous?" April continues to throw packages from the suitcase as June dodges them. "I'm the one that stayed to take care of a heartbroken mother, so thank you very much. Not to mention the piss and puke of old age."

Exhausted, April crumbles with emotion while June regains some composure.

"You may as well hear the rest of it," April says, quietly disturbed. "One day, after years of Mama's suffering, I turned the oxygen valve off instead of on. I did that."

June is stunned, silent.

April continues. "One little click up instead of down made such a significant difference." April collapses in agony onto the floor. She looks up tentatively at June.

The sisters stare at each other silently for a long moment. What passes between them is close to salvation. June embraces April, and years of exhaustion echo through April's wailing cries.

CHAPTER 57

June, April, and the baby sleep soundly as a unit on the bed. Pebbles ding the street-side French doors like popcorn. June rouses and peeks out the window. A burly white middle-aged man hurls rocks at the balcony.

June recognizes him immediately and shakes April awake. "It's Billy."

"Shit," April says, scrambling out of bed. "How did he find me?" April nods toward the baby. "Watch her."

On the balcony, April looks down at her husband. He holds his arms up as if to say, "Well?"

"I'm coming," April yells down to him. She quickly gets dressed and throws June a set of keys. "Mama's place needs some work, but it'll keep the rain off you two."

"Stop," June says. "Wait a minute, what are you saying? Where are you going?"

April holds her hand up, halting any further discussion. "Look, June, I just needed my sister, and she showed up. Let the rest of the nonsense go. What's done is done. Take care of *your* baby, and I hope to see you both at home. If you don't come back, I'll understand."

"What are you talkin' about?" June asks, incredulous and confused.

Billy's loud car horn screeches outside.

"I want you to raise that baby for me," April urges her sister. "It's the least you can do. After all, you ran off and left me to take care of Mama. Now it's your turn."

"Are you insane?" June shouts.

"I promise you," April continues, "I will have Billy stop at the first Baptist orphanage, and I will leave that sweet thing as sure as I'm standin' here. I will tell Billy it's yours, and I will leave the baby. I have plenty of crumb crunchers of my own, and they all favor their father. This one won't."

"But April—" June stutters.

"I mean it," April presses. "I'll give her away."

"Well," June retorts, "I'll probably do the exact same thing. I mean it too."

"It's your call," April shrugs without attachment and starts to exit. She pauses at the door and picks up a heavy gold necklace from the floor, the contents of one of several broken packages.

"How much is gold sellin' for these days?" she asks June. "All-time high, I do believe."

June shrugs, completely stunned at the change of subject.

April points to the packages. "I couldn't help myself. I peeked in one or two. You were generous with Mama. See ya, Sis." And with that, April bolts out the door.

June grabs a package and opens it. Three huge clumps of gold fall to the floor. June instantly recognizes the gold scarab bracelet from Cairo and the heavy gold necklace she bought in a bazaar in Istanbul. June laughs as she opens another box, and more gold jewelry tumbles out. She grabs the baby and rushes to the front balcony.

April climbs into the car with Billy, and June holds the baby up for them to see.

"Sunshine!" she yells.

April squints up at June.

"Her name is Sunshine!" June announces.

April smiles, and the sisters share a moment of unspoken agreement. April and Billy speed away toward home.

CHAPTER 58

June approaches her mother's shabby property. Growing up, June thought their family homestead was quaint, lovely, and historic. As an adult, the same rundown property now strikes her as a weary reminder of her mother's wilted dreams.

June rolls over a weedy gravel drive and parks in front of the old house. Sunshine, strapped into a car seat, sleeps in the back of the overloaded pink convertible. June surveys the empty acreage around the property, overgrown and shabby.

The homestead floods her with surprising emotion. Rather than recalling the old grief, guilt, and anger from her youth, June looks back at Sunshine. She translates the old feelings into a new hope instead. She knows that April was right. This home, the baby, a new life are exactly what she needed. It may take some work, but June knows this is where she belongs.

The years that follow are filled with hard work, care, and pride as June settles in and breathes new life into the old place. In the evenings, as she sips iced tea on the front porch while Sunshine chases lightning bugs in the yard, a few pleasant memories come to mind—

Sunshine coos in a swing as June weeds the garden.
Sunshine helps her mother paint a birdhouse.
June and Sunshine pick tomatoes in their well-manicured garden.
Sunshine colors in a coloring book on the front porch.

As Sunshine grows, mother and daughter begin to look nearly identical. The girl's coloring somehow matches that of June—olive skin, brown eyes, and auburn hair. One of their favorite activities together is sewing. They work in the evenings on a bright yellow quilt. Although Sunshine's small hands are not able to work the thread as June can, she's a wonderful helper, bringing June patches of material from an old chest of scraps that Alma collected.

On a warm summer afternoon, June and April sing to Sunshine as she blows out five birthday candles. April's gaze toward her daughter is that only of a loving aunt, nothing more. The whole family surrounds Sunshine, a watercolor of fun and happiness. The little girl rips into the strawberry cake, her favorite. Her dark-brown curls and olive skin contrast with her six pale and freckled cousins, who range in age from grade school to college.

April stands at the kitchen window, as she's done many times before. This time, she joyfully washes cake plates and watches her kids playing soccer in the yard. June brings in the last of the dishes. Sunshine trails her, with her small face covered in pink icing. June picks the girl up and sets her on the counter, grabbing a washcloth.

"Look at you, missy," June says to Sunshine, who squirms as June scrubs the icing from her face.

April smiles at her niece and tickles her. "Someone liked their cake today. That strawberry cake was your mother's favorite too."

"Yes, it was," June recalls fondly. "Every time your grandmother, Alma Mae, brought out the family recipe book, I begged her to make it."

Sunshine, not really knowing who the adults were talking about, simply grins and licks more pink icing off her fingers.

"Speaking of old things," April says, drying a plate and putting it away in the cupboard, "I saw you dragged Mama's old trunk out of her closet."

"Yeah," June says. She sets a wriggling but clean-faced Sunshine back on her feet. "I wanted you to help me look through some of the old photos and label them. I can't recall who's who anymore."

Sunshine scurries ahead of them and digs through the trunk, pulling out an old rag doll. She inspects the mildewed fabric and a missing glass eye and tosses it away almost instantly, returning to her coloring books on the coffee table.

April and June muddle through the trunk's contents and discover family photos, lace doilies, and various old keepsakes.

"Oh, my goodness, April," says June. She flips through a stack of church youth group pictures. "Look how pretty you were."

April takes a look. "Were?"

The sisters chuckle and commiserate over the old pictures.

Unnoticed by June and April, Sunshine pulls a cracked, worn leather diary from the trunk. She brings it over to the coffee table and, unaware of what the diary contains, colors over the cursive writing on the pages with a bright yellow crayon.

CHAPTER 59

That night, June tosses and turns in fitful sleep. She wakes to see a dark figure sitting on the foot of her bed. It has the shape of a man and whistles eerily. She bolts upright and turns the light on. The room is empty.

June rushes down the hallway to Sunshine's bedroom and frantically throws open the door. Her daughter sleeps peacefully under the yellow quilt, surrounded by an army of stuffed animals.

*　　*　　*

In the dark of night, a crude river raft floats in the misty water near a campsite with a large fire that illuminates the area. Mama Moo stirs a pot of stew over the fire, chanting to herself. *"Bah day, bah day, oh man jah ee! Ee! Oh, bah day, oh way, oh man jah ee!"*

Mama Moo serves herself a bowl of stew. Before she takes a bite, she freezes. Animal sounds and lapping water are all that she hears. But somewhere underneath the typical sounds of the swamp, she senses a presence. She smiles to herself and takes a large bite of stew.

Out of nowhere, a metal prosthetic hand clutches Mama Moo by the neck and lifts the old woman to her feet. The bowl and spoon drop from her hand. Mama, choking, merely smiles as she looks at Mister. She croaks out, "Hello, boy."

*   *   *

Up the river, June stands on her porch. Dressed in a flowing print with her natural brunette curls hanging around her shoulders, she is the antithesis of Miss June. June lets the night breeze flitter through her hair as she inhales deeply with contentment.

Just then, a barn owl hoots in a nearby tree as a brown snake slithers across her foot. She jumps back in shock, grabs a yard rake, and throws the snake into the yard. With a furrowed brow, she hobbles back inside the house, feeling uneasy. June locks the front door and closes all the windows. The wind rises outside. Something is coming.

*   *   *

On the river's edge, Mama Moo and Mister sit around the fire. Mama Moo is dressed shabbily while Mister sports a tailored suit. They act as if nothing volatile has just happened. Mama Moo shoves a bowl of stew into Mister's hands.

"You first," he tells Mama. "I just tried to choke you."

"But you couldn't," Mama retorts. Mama Moo smiles deviously and slurps from her own bowl, refilled. "What do you want?"

Mister laughs heartily and sniffs the air. "You stink, Mama. Take a bath."

"Funny how when God made you," she says, "he not only forgot your arm. He forgot your soul."

Mister spits at the ground. "I spit at heaven, old woman. You never trusted me with the knowledge, but I got it anyway."

Mama Moo, unfazed, stares at Mister for a long moment. "I should have chosen the girl."

Mister throws his bowl of hot stew at Mama Moo. She cackles in crazed laughter.

*   *   *

June quietly opens the door to Sunshine's room. She breathes a sigh of relief, confirming the girl is fast asleep. June pulls the yellow quilt up over Sunshine, whose brown hair splays over her pillow. As she turns to leave, June spots the leather diary nestled under a stuffed animal in the corner. She pulls it out and considers it for a moment.

"Oh, the trunk," June mutters to herself. She looks at Sunshine. "You little thief."

Casually, June opens the worn book and flips through the pages. Instantly, she recognizes the tight, curly penmanship of her mother, Alma Mae. June shakes her head as she notices many of the pages are covered in bright yellow crayon, but the writing is still visible.

June is about to close the diary for future reading when something catches her eye on the open page. Beneath a swipe of sheer yellow crayon, she reads:

The day was a blessing and a curse all in one. The little basket showed up on the porch steps. I could tell by the gimpy foot that the baby belonged to that witch by the river. She had a one-armed boy years before. And I knew who the baby's father was. I was married to him. God's revenge can be cruel.

June slams the diary shut.

CHAPTER 60

Five miles up the road, April stands at the sink in her own kitchen, washing the breakfast dishes. Through the kitchen window, she gazes at her daughters playing soccer outside. June and Sunshine pull up in the pink convertible, top down. Sunshine hops from the car and runs to play with her older cousins.

Without a second's delay, June angrily stomps into April's kitchen and slams their mother's diary on the breakfast table.

"Don't bring all that piss and vinegar into my house," April says in a warning tone.

"You knew, didn't you?" June spits.

"Knew what?" April says.

"You were only five years old, but you knew!" June says.

The look on April's face gives her the answer.

"Why didn't you tell me?" June asks.

The teapot whistles on the stove, giving April a moment to collect herself. She pours two cups of tea. "What would I do if I didn't have you to interrupt my dull life?"

"Everyone lied to me," June exclaims. "You all knew!"

"Secrets are a funny thing," April says, blowing on her hot tea. "They grow so scary that the fear of exposure becomes more sinister than the secret."

"How did Mama live with it?" June asks her.

"Sit down, June," April says.

June falls into a chair. April hands the teacup to June, who waves it away.

"Drink it," April urges. "It's your China tea, costs a fortune, remember?"

Reluctantly, June accepts the tea. "If I had known . . ." June said.

"If you had known," April responds, "then what? You would have left anyway! I say, so what? Dear ole' Dad was a philanderer. You were always Mama's favorite, anyway."

"Maybe I am just like them," June says tearfully. "No good."

"Who?" April asks.

"My *brother*, Mister," June hisses. "Our father. And the swamp witch."

"Oh honey, you are nothin' like them," April says. "You'll always be the brightest light in the room."

June shakes her head in defiance, then seems to move to distant thoughts as she begins to swirl her teacup around.

"Remember the story Aunt Beulah used to tell us about the walking catfish?" June says, closing her eyes.

"Yeah, it always freaked me out," April replies. "Those fish walked through the backyard on rainy days."

Suddenly, June has a vision. She sees Mama Moo's eyes and head, strangely blurred, like a watercolor painting.

April continues, "When Grampa trapped those weird walking fish in a garbage can, at first, they bloodied their heads trying to escape."

Behind her closed eyes, June's vision becomes clearer. Above the water's surface, she sees Mister holding Mama Moo's head under water. Mama Moo is drowning, yet she does not struggle.

April continues, "But then they wised up."

In her mind's eye, June watches as Mister releases Mama Moo—she floats, eyes closed, inches below the water's surface.

"They learned to play dead until Grampa removed the lid," April concludes.

In June's vision, under the water, Mama Moo's eyes open wide. And so do June's.

"And only then," June finishes the story for April, "would they come back to life and escape."

June's hand trembles as she sets down her teacup and bolts, without explanation, from April's kitchen. Over her shoulder she yells, "Watch Sunshine. Keep her here."

Stunned, April nods her consent and watches her sister drive away.

CHAPTER 61

June struggles to carry a heavy bucket. Carefully, she pours a thin line of red sand around the perimeter of her house. A barn owl and hawk screech three times and fly to the north. A warning of impending danger.

The wind picks up as June stares into the setting sun. She finds herself mesmerized by the pink, orange, and yellow stripes that sink into the river and eventually turn to darkness. She steels herself for what she knows is to come in the night.

In her living room, June pulls voodoo candles from a shelf. She places a candle in each of the four corners of the room, as well as on the fireplace hearth, and lights them. A bundle of sage emits a stream of gray smoke. June carries the bundle through the living room and kitchen as she smudges the area in a ritual cleansing.

She chants and covers the mirror over the fireplace with a sheet. *"Bah day, bah day, oh man jah ee! Oh, bah day, oh way, oh man jah ee!"*

June chants as she arranges an altar on the mantle, which displays freshly baked bread, a pack of cigarettes, a shot of whiskey, fresh white flowers, a bell, and a statue of Mary. The altar is an offering to the voodoo gods.

After the saging and the altar is complete, June draws a chalk circle on the wood floor. In the middle of the circle, she draws a cross. She places a single chair on the cross and a second chair opposite. Before she goes to her bedroom for final preparations, June visits each and every door and window in her home and opens them wide, inviting the mystery to enter.

*   *   *

Night has fallen. A light breeze flirts with the window sheers in June's bedroom. It's time for her strongest ritual. June buttons herself into a crisp, white dress. She removes her shoes and places them neatly under the bed. This part of the process makes June nervous, as she's off balance without her raised shoe. June hobbles to the dresser and removes a long white scarf from the drawer. In the mirror, she watches herself wrap the scarf like a turban around her head, covering her hair.

Next, June hangs an ornate antique necklace with a silver amulet around her neck. She opens the amulet and confirms it is filled with translucent white cemetery dust. She screws it shut. June retrieves her gift from Pearl—the gold Bible—that lies on the vanity and clutches it to her chest. In the full-length mirror, June looks at herself. Satisfied with her appearance, she intentionally covers the mirror with a sheet to prevent entry by unwanted spirits.

June's preparations are all in effect. A roaring fire warms the living room, candles are lit, and June takes her place in the center chair. She closes her eyes. Her hands rest gently on the Bible laying in her lap. She waits.

From outside, eerie whistling floats into the room on a breeze, followed by heavy footsteps crackling over the gravel. Mister walks in through the open front door.

Although she's been expecting this, June winces at his sudden entrance. He takes his place in the chair opposite June.

"I have something you lost," Mister hisses, pulling June's gold cross necklace from his pocket.

June opens her eyes but does not react. Whatever sadness June feels about seeing the necklace she gave to Maxine is quickly set aside. She cannot afford to lose focus.

In his chair, Mister removes a leather pouch and opens it. With prosthetic fingers, he clumsily dips the gold cross into the pouch. When he pulls it out, it is covered in translucent white dust.

"Expensive stuff," June says.

Mister shrugs. "What price will men pay for power?"

Mister removes a voodoo doll that resembles June and her short leg. Without warning, he stabs the doll using the gold cross as a pin.

June closes her eyes and remains still. For a moment, Mister cannot tell if she is breathing. Suddenly, with a loud animal howl, June opens her eyes. Mister is stunned at the force of June's energy.

"You have to have pure intention for the dust to work," June announces with strength. She quickly opens the silver amulet hanging around her neck and pours cemetery dust onto her palm. With a powerful breath, she blows the dust at Mister. It lands on his legs like powdery snow.

For a moment, nothing happens. Mister laughs and breathes a sigh of relief. A second later, Mister's legs begin to tremble. His face melts into pain and fear. With his prosthetic hand, he lifts his pant leg to see dozens of leeches covering both legs. The slimy creatures writhe and wriggle from knees to ankles and attempt to burrow into his skin.

Unbidden, Mister screams and empties his entire pouch of dust onto his legs. The leeches freeze and dissolve into thin air. Infuriated, Mister leaps from his chair and barrels toward June.

With swift action, June opens the gold Bible and removes a small handgun hidden inside—Pearl's true gift. She shoots, but her aim is off. A bullet ricochets off of Mister's prosthetic arm and sends sparks flying across the room.

Stunned, Mister halts in his tracks and stares at his damaged prosthetic limb. Red with rage, he flies through the air with incredible force toward June. She scrambles from her chair to avoid the massive, raging man.

June fires once more and hits Mister in the leg, causing it to spill blood. Mister falls into June, knocking her backward onto the fireplace hearth. The gun flies from her hand and lands directly in the middle of the roaring fire. This weapon is lost to her.

In an instant, Mister is on top of June, choking her with his natural hand. June reaches behind her, grabs one of the lit candles, and smashes flame and hot wax into Mister's face. The pain forces Mister to release his grip for just a moment.

As he does, June kicks him off and jumps to her feet. She grabs the fire poker and takes a swing at Mister. She misses.

Mister sees the burning gun smoldering inside the roaring fire. Mister and June lock eyes for an instant. Before June can make another move, Mister reaches through the flames with his prosthetic hand and grabs the gun. The gleam in Mister's eye renews June's fortitude. She must fight.

June scrambles to escape, but Mister trips her. June falls with a moan and lies helpless, face first on the floor. Mister steps on her back with a heavy boot, pinning her down.

He points the gun at her head. "Bye bye, Sister," he snarls.

For a split second, time freezes. June's mind wanders back to Sunshine's first smile, back to her old French Quarter apartment. She and April were delighted to see the baby had a beautiful dimple. June is dragged back to the present by a loud crack.

As Mister fires the gun, an iron skillet descends upon his head. Mister crumples immediately to the ground next to June, sending the bullet astray, barely missing June's head. Blood gushes from Mister's skull. June flips quickly over to see Mama Moo towering above her son, holding the skillet.

June tries to sit up, but she is dizzy. June and Mama Moo lock eyes for only a moment. A lifetime passes between the two women. The connection is broken as June passes out.

*　　*　　*

Hours later, as dawn breaks over the riverbank, June finally wakes. Her back is stiff and her head throbs. She sits up and realizes she's on the couch.

June rubs her eyes and looks around the room. Everything is in its proper place again. There is no sign of the chairs, the chalk circle, or the candles. All of her preparations from the night before are gone.

It's as if nothing ever happened. Was she dreaming? She has a fleeting vision of Mama Moo's dark eyes, but she can't hold the memory.

June heads for the kitchen to make coffee to clear her head. On the mantle of the fireplace, something glitters and catches her eye. She picks up her gold cross necklace and clasps it around her neck. In an instant, she remembers exactly what happened last night.

CHAPTER 62

Mama Moo hovers over Mister's dead body in the darkness. She has spent the last night and all day preparing his body. She lovingly kisses his forehead and moves a lock of hair away from his closed eyes. A single tear runs down her cheek.

Mama Moo steps back and surveys her son's body. He now lies on their wooden raft. The raft they once called home for so many years. Mama Moo soaks the body and raft with gasoline.

"Choices. Always your choices," Mama Moo mutters. "You made me choose one over the other. Why? Even that day, you chose to give away your baby sister to those folks up the hill."

Mama Moo wades into the dark river. The murky water is lit only by the full moon overhead. She pushes the raft deeper toward the river's current.

"What you didn't know," she continues, "was that man was father to you both. Maybe if I'd told you, things might have been different."

Mama Moo lights a match. Her hand shakes in resistance. "A mother shouldn't have to choose between her children."

She throws the match onto the raft, setting it ablaze. "This time, boy, you left me no choice."

The raft ignites fiercely in a ball of flame. The sky reflects orange as the raft disappears into the darkness of the river. Mama Moo wades in deeper and deeper until fully submerged. Once she can go no further, she sinks into the dark water, performing her own baptism and washing away her sin.

The dark water closes in upon her.

CHAPTER 63

Three Months Later

On a beautiful fall day, June and April sip iced tea in rockers on June's porch while Sunshine plays in the yard.

"Pearl's coming for a visit next week," June tells her sister. "You know, after the judge's death, the entire estate reverted to Pearl, no more problems. She's opened the house and cemetery to anyone in need. Last count, four families were there."

"What happened to that handsome brother of hers?" April asks friskily.

"April," June rolls her eyes. "You're a married woman."

April smiles knowingly. "Now, you know very well I'd have to collect a lot of change to make bus fare to Italy, wouldn't I?"

June hands a colorful envelope to April. She pulls out a tropical postcard and a wad of cash. "What gives?" April asks.

"It's from Jay. He bought a bar in Mexico," June chuckles.

"With your money?" April retorts.

June nods. "He wants me to join him."

"I'm sure he does," April says.

June scoffs. "That pissant had the nerve to say he did it 'for us.'"

April straightens her posture, disturbed.

"No," June says. "I'm not going."

April lets out her breath. "Good, 'cause I think you could do some good around here. This parish needs someone like you, Miss June."

The sisters sip their tea from China, united in the moment. They watch Sunshine in the distance chasing butterflies. Eventually, the little girl runs back to her mother and aunt. She hands June a brilliant red flower with a star-shaped blue center.

"Thank you, Sunshine," June says. "This is a lovely flower. Very unusual."

April looks at the strange flower. "You can tell it's a very special flower, Sunshine."

The little girl looks dismayed. "I'm sorry, Aunt April, the lady only gave me one."

"What lady?" June asks.

Sunshine looks from June to April and shrugs. "She told me her name was Mama Moo."

June and April exchange a knowing look. Sunshine skips back out into the yard. The farmhouse shrinks into the distance as a hawk watches from a faraway perch. The great bird screeches three times and flies to the north.

THE END

ABOUT THE AUTHOR

Every T.E. Lane story begins with family at its core and spirals into mystery, action, and a touch of the supernatural. It's a place where magic always feels possible, the coincidences may not be so coincidental, and the line between reality and something more is always worth crossing.

T.E. Lane writes screenplays and fiction. A fan of action, thriller, mystery, and literary fiction, the author enjoys blending aspects of many genres into a single work, creating a unique reading experience that will keep you turning the pages. Connect with the author on social media @telane_author.

IngramElliott Publishing

IngramElliott is an award-winning independent publisher with a mission to bring great stories to light in print and on-screen. We publish stories with a unique voice that will translate well into film and television. Visit us at www.ingramelliott.com for more information.

Our *IngramElliott* imprint features full-length fiction and nonfiction titles designed with the book lover in mind.

Our *IE Snaps!* imprint features novella-length fiction in popular genres that are designed for a quick read on the go.